MY CO-STAR, MY ENEMY

When the tape was finished, Mr. Greenspan looked at Alison with a grin. "Like I said, you're a natural."

"I am?" Alison whispered.

"I know you think this is crazy. Heck, a part of me thinks it's crazy. There's plenty of professional actresses who would jump at this job." Now Mr. Greenspan was pacing the office, waving his hands excitedly. "But as Kate can testify, I've always had a knack for picking out new faces. I'm offering you the job of Jane on Sticks and Stones.*"*

The room suddenly felt very hot. "My parents . . ." Alison said weakly.

"Oh, of course, you have to talk to them. Or do you want me to?" Mr. Greenspan grinned. "So how does it feel, Alison?" he asked. "You're going to be a star."

My Co-Star, My Enemy

HOLLYWOOD WARS

My Co-Star, My Enemy

ILENE COOPER

PUFFIN BOOKS

PUFFIN BOOKS
Published by the Penguin Group
Penguin Books USA Inc., 375 Hudson Street, New York, New York 10014, U.S.A.
Penguin Books Ltd, 27 Wrights Lane, London W8 5TZ, England
Penguin Books Australia Ltd, Ringwood, Victoria, Australia
Penguin Books Canada Ltd, 10 Alcorn Avenue, Toronto, Ontario, Canada M4V 3B2
Penguin Books (N.Z.) Ltd, 182–190 Wairau Road, Auckland 10, New Zealand

Penguin Books Ltd, Registered Offices: Harmondsworth, Middlesex, England

First published in the United States of America by Puffin Books,
a division of Penguin Books USA Inc., 1993

1 3 5 7 9 10 8 6 4 2

LIBRARY OF CONGRESS CATALOGING-IN-PUBLICATION DATA
Cooper, Ilene.   My co-star, my enemy / Ilene Cooper.
p.   cm.—(Hollywood wars; #1)
Summary: Temperaments clash on the set when veteran child actress
Jamie and sheltered rich girl Alison are cast as the stars of a new
television series.
ISBN 0-14-036156-1
[1. Television—Production and direction—Fiction.]   I. Title.
II. Series: Cooper, Ilene.   Hollywood wars; #1.
PZ7.C7856My   1993   [Fic]—dc20   92-39515

Printed in the United States of America
Set in Times Roman

High-Flyer™ is a trademark of Puffin Books, a division of Penguin Books USA Inc.

My Co-Star, My Enemy

Chapter 1

"Will you please tell me what I'm doing here?" Alison Blake demanded. She looked over at her friend Dana Jones, who was tensely gripping the steering wheel of her mother's convertible.

"Ali, please, I'm trying to change lanes. I haven't changed lanes that many times in my life."

Perfect, Alison thought. *Not only am I on a wild goose chase, I might not even get there in one piece.*

"Okay," Dana finally said, letting out a relieved breath. "I can stay here all the way to Century City. Now what did you want?"

"I want to know why you need me to go to this audition with you. You've been on them before."

"But this is the first time I've had a real appointment with a real producer. The others were just cattle calls."

"Cattle calls?"

"You know, a bunch of people just show up for the

interview. Anyone can come. But my drama teacher set this one up. Do you realize how important this could be?"

"All I know is you grabbed me after study hall and said, 'Come on.' What am I going to do? Why am I here?"

"I guess I got scared," Dana admitted sheepishly. "I didn't want to go alone."

Alison stared at her friend. Dana scared? That was usually her own role. Goody-goody Alison, afraid to do anything. The top of the car was down, and it whipped Alison's reddish gold hair over her shoulder. She really wanted to get her hair cut, to stop looking so much like a fifteen-year-old Alison Wonderland, but whenever she mentioned it to her parents, her father always protested, "You look so sweet with your hair long."

She was getting awfully tired of being described as sweet, though she supposed the adjective was accurate. Wishy-washy might also be accurate. That was one reason she liked Dana so much. Dana had a mind of her own. She knew she wanted to get into acting, and here she was doing something about it. Alison couldn't see much past her next history test.

A car full of boys pulled up beside them. The driver honked and waved at Alison. "Hey, I think I love you," he called.

Alison turned her head, and the boy gunned past them. "Creeps," she muttered.

"I don't get it," Dana said. "A gorgeous thing like you, you should be used to a few stares."

"I'm not. Gorgeous, I mean."

"Well, you would be if you paid more attention to yourself." Dana took her eyes off the road long enough to give Alison a critical glance. "You have all the requirements. That great hair, huge blue eyes, the bod of a model—"

"Dana . . ." Embarrassed, Alison cut her off.

"But you don't *do* anything with all that good stuff. No makeup, boring clothes . . ."

"I'm wearing jeans and a white shirt, just like plenty of other girls at school," Alison protested.

"Not the same at all. The sleeves are supposed to be rolled up. The jeans are supposed to be torn. Yours are pressed, for pete's sake."

"Hey, if I'm such a geek, maybe I shouldn't go with you. It might rub off," Alison said, half-amused and half-hurt.

"Hah!" Dana retorted. "You're not getting out of this that easily. Start looking for the exit, okay?"

Alison started looking. She knew Dana needed all the help she could get. Alison had her permit, and she had gone out driving with her mom twice. It was just enough to show her how much there was to think about while she was trying to concentrate on the road.

"There. Get off there." Alison pointed as the exit suddenly loomed.

Dana stepped on the gas and flew across two lanes. Alison held her breath until Dana had safely exited and was headed toward the Century City complex.

"What time is it?" Dana asked.

"Three-thirty," Alison told her. This was Dana's big appointment but, as usual, she wasn't even wearing a watch.

"I'm early."

"Well, let's park and get our bearings." Century City was a big complex with movie theaters, shops, and apartments, as well as office buildings. It took a little hunting, but finally they found the building where Twilight Productions was located.

"How do I look?" Dana asked, as they rode up in the elevator.

"Perfect. That dress is perfect," Alison assured her. "Not like anything *I'd* wear," she added.

If Dana caught Alison's sarcasm, she didn't comment. When the elevator doors opened, she rifled through her purse for a mirror and ran her fingers through her short dark hair.

"Okay, let's go," she said, putting on a dazzling smile.

They walked into a large office tastefully decorated in mauves and grays. Girls of all shapes and sizes crammed the reception area.

"I didn't think there would be this many," Dana whispered.

"Can I help you?" the cool, blonde receptionist asked.

"Dana Jones. I'm here for the audition with Mr. Greenspan."

"Of course," the receptionist replied in a bored

voice. She checked a list, then looked up at Alison. "What about you?"

"Oh no. I'm just . . . um . . . here with my friend."

The receptionist rolled her eyes, as if bringing along a friend was the most unprofessional thing she'd ever heard of, but all she said was, "Do you have photos?"

Dana handed her the manila envelope she had been clutching. Alison knew it held the composite pictures that all actors and actresses needed. There were ten large sheets showing Dana in different poses: head shots, full body poses, Dana laughing, Dana serious. Even these were distilled down from fifty or more shots a professional photographer had taken. Alison knew because she had looked at every single one of the fifty—over and over.

The receptionist took the envelope and put it on top of a stack. "Have a seat."

That was easier said than done. Every chair seemed to be taken.

"You sit," Alison said. "Maybe I should just go downstairs and wait."

"No. We can both squeeze in on that couch."

A serious-looking girl with horn-rimmed glasses frowned as Alison and Dana tried to make themselves comfortable next to her.

"Distract me. Talk about something," Dana implored.

Alison thought for a few seconds. "I think Steve is going to ask you to the prom."

"Oh, fine topic, Ali."

"Steve's a good guy," Alison protested. "He's cute and nice and—"

"And that's about it," Dana finished. "Yawn. He does not interest me. Period."

Alison knew that pleading Steve Kaye's case was probably a losing proposition. Steve had a crush on Dana that was so big even the school janitor probably knew about it, but Dana clearly couldn't care less.

"If you like Steve so much, why don't you date him?" Dana challenged, then answered her own question. "Because you have an awesome boyfriend, that's why. You and hunky Brad D'amato." Dana shook her head. "Go figure."

A comment like that from anyone else would have gotten Alison angry, but outspoken Dana had been speaking her mind to Alison ever since fourth grade. Besides, in this case, Alison secretly agreed with her. She wasn't sure why Brad had picked her to ask out about six months ago.

Brad and Alison couldn't be more opposite. He was always ready for anything—the wilder and more outrageous, the better. Alison was different. It wasn't just that she always followed the rules. She actually liked following rules. She liked the orderliness of it all. Her schoolwork was important to her, and she was proud of her good grades. Brad just wanted grades good enough to keep him on the football team.

Half the time, Alison felt like she was a drag on

him—especially when she couldn't help scolding him about dull stuff, like homework and upcoming tests. But Brad kept asking her out, and Alison had to admit she enjoyed having one of the coolest boys in school to herself.

Dana tapped her foot nervously and then picked out a magazine from several that were scattered around the coffee table in front of them. Obviously, she was going to try and distract herself. Alison, on the other hand, was content to look around. She had nothing to worry about. She might as well scope out Dana's competition.

None of the girls seemed familiar. She had thought that she might recognize a few actresses in the room. Now Alison wondered if they were all novices like Dana. Glancing sideways at the girl next to her, Alison decided she didn't seem like the right type to be on a television show at all. Why, she was downright plain. There was a pixieish girl sitting across the room who was kind of cute, but nothing special. The rest were all good-looking, but none of them was what you'd call really beautiful.

Then a redheaded girl sitting in a corner caught her eye. She was far prettier than the rest of the hopefuls and had a presence about her that made her stand out of the crowd.

"What are you looking at?" Dana whispered.

"Who. That girl over there." Alison gestured slightly with her head. "She looks familiar. Has she been in something?"

Dana peered at the girl. "Wasn't she on that show, *The Happydale Girls*?"

"That's it. I used to love that show when I was little."

"It's still on sometimes in reruns."

Alison tried to remember a few more details about the girl. "I think she played Mimi."

"They made that show years ago. I wonder what she's been doing lately?"

The girl looked up as if she sensed Alison and Dana were talking about her. She stared at them defiantly.

Alison picked up a magazine. She didn't want to be rude and just gawk. She had to admit, though, that spotting a real-life actress gave this whole escapade a new air of excitement.

Maybe she was glad she had come along after all.

Chapter 2

I wonder what those two were saying about me, Jamie O'Leary thought to herself. From the way they both had guiltily started reading when she caught them, it was obvious that she'd been the topic of their whispering. *Oh, who cares?* Jamie thought. If they were the competition, she didn't have a thing to worry about. After working in television for so many years, she could spot amateurs a mile away.

She tossed her copper-colored hair, fixed today in a neat and sophisticated french braid, over her shoulder. Then, she smoothed the skirt of her plaid, sleeveless dress. Though it was neatly pressed, it looked as old as it was. At least her red flats and shiny red leather belt were new. Usually, she just handed the money she made as a checker at the grocery store over to her mother. But knowing this important audition was coming up, she had held out some of her last paycheck to buy some accessories she hoped would spruce up her one decent outfit.

Taking a deep breath, Jamie realized just how nervous she was. This was her first audition in years. Six and a half years, to be exact. When she'd left *The Happydale Girls,* she had no idea it was going to be such a long time between jobs.

On *The Happydale Girls,* a comedy about five girls living in an orphanage, Jamie had played the role of Mimi, the youngest, most mischievous orphan. She'd started the show when she was four. But at the ripe old age of nine, as one of the producers had so bluntly put it, she got "officially stuck in an awkward phase." It was a remark that had burned itself into Jamie's brain. By that time, the show was running out of steam anyway. The ratings were down, and the story lines weren't as funny as they had been in the early years. So the show was canceled, and though her mother had assured her she would get another job quickly, none had materialized. Jamie had felt terrible, like a pre-teen failure. After a while, she had refused to go on any more interviews. She just couldn't take the rejection.

Only recently, at her mother's insistence, had she gotten professional pictures taken.

"Start making the rounds again," Mrs. O'Leary implored. "You're so beautiful now. And you've always been a natural actress. Don't waste your talent like I did."

They had scraped together the money for the pictures, and Jamie had sent them to several agents. Meg Wildman, who remembered her from *The Happydale Girls,* decided to take a chance and signed her on as a client. After what seemed like months of not much happening, Meg had finally heard about this new show and made arrangements for the producers to see Jamie.

Now that she was sitting here, Jamie realized how important it was that she get this job. She wanted to show all of Hollywood that she wasn't some kid flash in the pan. But there were also far more practical reasons why she desperately needed this part.

Jamie glanced at her watch. Four o'clock. Her appointment was for three-thirty, and she'd been sitting here for over a half hour already. Should she go up to that witchy receptionist and ask her what was going on, or would that be too pushy? She didn't want to ruin her chances, but on the other hand, just waiting around for something to happen was horrible. If they didn't call her soon, she'd be a wreck by the time the producers actually asked her to speak some lines.

Glancing toward the producer's office, Jamie saw a tall man with frizzy hair and aviator glasses standing in the doorway. He was looking around the room, as if sizing up the hopefuls. She watched as his eyes lit on the girl with the long, red hair reading a magazine, the one who had been so interested in her. He whispered something to the receptionist, who shook her head and murmured a reply in his ear.

The producer went back to his office. Jamie settled back into her chair, but before she could get too comfortable, the receptionist called, "Jamie O'Leary."

Jamie stood up and smoothed her dress once more.

"Mr. Greenspan will see you now." The receptionist gestured toward the door.

Taking a deep breath, Jamie pasted a smile on her face and walked in.

The man with the frizzy hair stood up to shake her hand. "Hello, Jamie. I'm Dan Greenspan, the executive producer of *Sticks and Stones.*"

"How do you do?" Jamie hoped her grip was strong and confident.

An attractive African American woman in her late thirties was sitting in a leather chair alongside Mr. Greenspan's impressive chrome and glass desk. "And I'm Kate Morton. I'm the head writer." Her warm smile made Jamie relax. A little.

"Have a seat, Jamie," Mr. Greenspan invited.

Jamie sat down and crossed her legs demurely at the ankles. She remembered from her long-ago appearances on talk shows that this was the ladylike way to sit.

Mr. Greenspan scanned her résumé and shuffled through her photographs. Then he looked up. "I certainly remember you from your days as Mimi. You were quite the little ham."

Did that comment call for a thank you? It didn't exactly sound like a compliment. But apparently Mr.

Greenspan had meant it that way. "You sure knew how to play to the camera," he added approvingly.

"I gained a lot of wonderful experience. I was on the show for six years." There. That should remind him she wasn't just one of the nobodies sitting in his outer office.

Mr. Greenspan leaned back in his chair. "What have you been doing lately? Can I see you anywhere?"

Yep, she thought, *I'm appearing every day after school at Ralph's Market.* "I decided to stay out of the business after *The Happydale Girls* was canceled. I wanted a more normal life." That's what she said out loud. To herself she added silently, *If you call living in a tiny apartment over a Chinese restaurant in a crummy neighborhood* normal.

Mr. Greenspan talked with her for a few more minutes, mentioning some of the people she had worked with on *Happydale.* By the time the chitchat was over, Jamie felt slightly more at ease.

"Do you know anything about *Sticks and Stones*?" Kate Morton asked, moving the conversation toward the reason for the interview.

"My agent told me it was a sitcom about families."

"Let me tell you the story," Kate said enthusiastically. "It's about two families coming together. Joe Stickley is a widower with two children, a pretty teenage daughter and her slightly older brother. Joe owns a garage in a suburb of Chicago, and though he is just an average guy, Joe's got lots of rich clients who bring in their Mercedes and BMWs. One of them is Amanda Stone. Amanda's divorced. Her daughter is about the same age as Joe's, and she also has a precocious little boy. Naturally, Joe and Amanda get together, but the kids aren't too enthusiastic about it."

"Lots of problems mixing the two families?" Jamie suggested.

"Oh yes. With one family very rich and the other middle class, and all those kids, well, there's lots of opportunity for funny, interesting stuff," Mr. Greenspan replied.

"I can't mention any names right now, because the contracts aren't all worked out," Ms. Morton said, "but we've tapped two very big stars to play Joe and Amanda."

"What part am I up for?" Jamie asked hesitantly.

"We're not sure yet," Mr. Greenspan told her.

If one's rich and one's poor, I know which one I'll probably get, Jamie thought. But who cared? Any role on this show would be wonderful. Heck, she'd even play the bratty little brother. A wave of longing swept over Jamie. She had never wanted anything more than to be on *Sticks and Stones.*

"Are you ready to do a little reading?" Ms. Morton asked. "I have a sample script right here."

Jamie took it nervously. "Can I have a few moments to look it over?"

Mr. Greenspan nodded. "Certainly."

Jamie quickly scanned the script. The part she was reading for was rich Mrs. Stone's daughter, Wendy.

Wendy was having an argument with her little brother about who was going to walk their big Irish wolfhound.

Mr. Greenspan took the role of the little brother. At first it was slightly disconcerting having to pretend this middle-aged guy was a nine-year-old, but she just pictured him without his glasses, wearing short pants, and it seemed to work. Even though she hadn't had enough time to properly study the script, Jamie could see where the funny parts were and played them to the hilt. She could feel the old adrenalin flowing as she really got into the scene. She was acting again, and it felt wonderful.

When she put down the script, she looked at Mr. Greenspan confidently. She hoped for a smile at least, but couldn't tell a thing from his impassive expression. Hadn't she done well? He ought to know how vulnerable actors and actresses were. Jamie sure did. They were always waiting for someone—producers, critics, the audience—to tell them that they had done a good job. And that's what she was doing right now.

"That was quite a spirited reading, Jamie," Mr. Greenspan finally said with a brief, businesslike nod.

"Very nice," Ms. Morton added enthusiastically.

Jamie looked at her gratefully.

Mr. Greenspan rose. "Thank you for coming in."

This was it, apparently. Jamie tried to hide her disappointment. Her big chance was over, and she'd blown it. "Thank you for seeing me," she answered automatically as she stood up to go.

"Don't look so worried, Jamie." Mr. Greenspan's tone was unexpectedly kind.

She glanced up at him. "Pardon me?"

"You really did a very fine job. I didn't mean to rush you out. I just have so many more girls to interview."

"I understand. . . . It's just that . . ." She didn't want to sound too needy.

He came around the desk and patted her on the shoulder. "We *will* be in touch," he promised.

"Thanks," she said, trying to smile.

Alison watched the *Happydale* girl walk out of the office. She didn't look as if she had just landed the role. *If a professional actress like her couldn't make it, what chance did Dana have,* Alison thought worriedly.

Another girl was called in for her interview. Dana looked over at Alison. "I'm getting crazy."

"It won't be much longer," Alison said sympathetically. But the minutes dragged on.

"When are they going to call me?" Dana asked. It sounded more like a moan.

"Soon. See. There's that man talking to the receptionist. Oh my goodness, he's walking over here."

Mr. Greenspan stood in front of them. "I'm Dan Greenspan, the executive producer. I understand you're not here for the audition."

"Yes, I am," Dana replied, confused.

"I didn't mean you, dear. I meant your friend. Are you an actress?" he asked Alison.

Alison looked nervously at Dana. Mr. Greenspan was waiting for an answer.

"No, I'm just here with Dana."

"Well, I'd like to talk to you anyway."

"Me?" Alison squeaked.

"It won't take long. If you wouldn't mind?"

Alison again glanced at Dana, who seemed in shock. Well, what could she say? *No, I'm too busy reading a magazine?* "I guess we can talk."

"Good. Come into my office."

Alison obediently followed him and took the seat Mr. Greenspan indicated. He introduced her to the head writer and then said, "I guess you're wondering what this is all about."

"Yes."

Mr. Greenspan put his hands together. "Did you see the girl with the plaid dress who auditioned earlier?"

Alison nodded. "She used to be on that show *The Happydale Girls,* didn't she?"

"Yes. She's Jamie O'Leary. She was quite good. We auditioned her for one of the teenage roles on our new show. I had already seen you in the waiting room. You have just the look I want for one of the girls, and when Jamie came in with her red hair, I thought, Wouldn't it be great if I could get the two of you on the show? Both redheads, but one a fiery, sarcastic kid, and the other sweet and angelic."

Alison wasn't quite sure she understood. "You mean, you want me to audition?"

"I certainly do. Have you done any acting at all?"

"Just school plays and stuff," Alison replied with embarrassment. It sounded lame even to her own ears.

"Well, that's something. Look," he said bluntly. "You could be lousy but, like I said, you're just the type I want. I haven't offered Jamie the job yet, but it's likely I will. If you're any good, I think you two could be dynamite together."

Alison felt as if she was in a dream, but she wasn't sure if it was a good one or a nightmare. *Calm down,* she told herself. *This is ridiculous. You're no actress. You'll read for the part, he'll say thank you, never mind, and you will leave.*

"Let me tell you a little about the plot and the characters," Mr. Greenspan was saying.

She could barely keep her mind on what he was telling her. The garage owner, the divorcée, their children; it was all getting mixed up in her head.

Ms. Morton handed her a script. "Look it over, you're reading the part of Jane."

Trying to keep her mind on the words, Alison went over the dialogue. Jane and her boyfriend were trying to decide if they should go to a movie or out to dinner. Well, this all seemed pretty straightforward. She had had this discussion with Brad a million times.

"Alison," Ms. Morton broke in gently. "We're running short on time. Are you ready to try it?"

Alison nodded. As ready as she'd ever be. Mr. Greenspan took the part of the boyfriend. A funny thing happened as she got into the part. She forgot that she was nervous, that she was sitting in a television producer's office, even that the person in front of her was Mr. Greenspan, not a teenager. Suddenly, the whole scene seemed very real to her. She wanted to go to the movie, not out to a Mexican restaurant where, as the script said, "everything contained beans, even the cokes."

It was a long piece, but finally she was done reading. She put her script down on the desk, still high from the excitement of acting.

Mr. Greenspan was looking at Ms. Morton. "Like finding Lana Turner at the drug store," he informed her.

"Who's Lana Turner?" Alison asked shyly.

Dan Greenspan turned to her and laughed. "Oh, a big star in the forties. Way before your time. She was sitting at the counter of Schwab's Drug Store when a talent agent found her."

"Oh." *Oh!* He was comparing her to this Lana Turner? Did that mean he liked her? Alison didn't have to wait to find out.

"You're a natural, Alison. You sounded just great."

Alison didn't know whether she should admit that the dialogue hadn't been all that much of a stretch.

"I think we'd like to have you do a video test," Ms. Morton said, "just to see how you look on camera."

"Now?"

"There's an editing suite a few offices down. We can do it there."

"But . . . but . . ."

"I know this all seems as if it's happening very quickly," Mr. Greenspan said, "but we want to get things moving."

"My friend . . ." Alison said faintly.

"We'll tell her what's happening. If she wants to wait, that will be fine."

"But I'll be late getting home."

"You can call your parents, can't you?" Mr. Greenspan asked. "Tell them what's going on."

Alison knew her parents weren't home. That would be a fine message to leave on the machine. "Mom, Dad, I've gotten a role in a television show. See you when I see you." Oh, well, she supposed she could just say the auditions were running late.

Before she knew what was going on, she made her phone call and left a vague message about being late, spoke briefly to Dana, who said through clenched teeth that she would wait, and was hustled off to a nearby office, where she was taken into a room with overhead lights and video cameras.

A young man greeted her. "Have you ever done this before?" he asked.

"Made a videotape? Not unless you count the stuff my dad shoots at Christmas."

"Hardly," he answered with a smile. "Here's what I want you to do. First, sit on that stool and start talking to me."

"About what?" she asked, starting to feel panicky all over again.

"Anything you want. Tell me what you did today."

She seated herself on the stool. "Well, it's been a really weird day." She launched into her amazing adventure, finishing with, "and now, here I am making a videotape."

"Boy, you're one lucky kid," the young man commented. "Do you know how many girls would kill for a chance like this?"

She sure did. And one of them, named Dana, was cooling her heels in Mr. Greenspan's office, waiting for her to get done.

"Now, walk around the room for me."

Self-consciously, Alison did what she was told.

"All right, you're finished. That wasn't too painful, was it?"

Alison wasn't sure. She didn't know what she was feeling by now.

Back in Mr. Greenspan's office, he popped the tape into his video machine. Alison could barely stand to look. There she was, chattering on in what seemed a very high voice about her whole long dumb day. Well, this should clinch it. He'd never want her now.

But when the tape was finished, Mr. Greenspan looked at her with a grin. "Like I said, you're a natural."

"I am?" Alison whispered.

"I know you think this is crazy. Heck, a part of me thinks it's crazy. There's plenty of professional actresses who would jump at this job." Now Mr. Greenspan was pacing the office, waving his hands excitedly. "But as Kate can testify, I've always had a knack for picking out new faces. I'm offering you the job of Jane on *Sticks and Stones*."

The room suddenly felt very hot. "My parents . . ." Alison said weakly.

"Oh, of course, you have to talk to them. Or do you want me to?"

"I . . . I'll do it."

"Then I'll phone them later tonight, explain all the details." He frowned. "Perhaps it would be better if I came by. About eight?"

"That would be good." Alison was sure she was going to need some backup. Besides, if Mr. Greenspan didn't come by, her parents might think she'd lost her mind and hallucinated the whole thing.

Mr. Greenspan grinned. "So, how does it feel, Alison?" he asked. "You're going to be a star!"

Chapter 3

Still reeling, Alison walked into the now-empty waiting room and sat down on the couch.

"Will you please tell me what's going on?" Dana demanded.

"I was offered a part in the television show."

For a few seconds, Dana just stared at her friend. Then she said, "*They* actually *told* you *you* had a *part?*"

Alison just nodded.

"Well." That was all Dana could say. "Well."

Quickly, Alison told her how it had all come about. Now that this was starting to seem real, excitement colored her voice. She was so into the story, she didn't notice that Dana remained pretty silent except for an occasional "uh-huh."

When she was finished, Alison took a deep breath. "I can't believe it. Can you?"

"No," Dana said flatly.

Alison focused in on her friend. No wonder Dana

couldn't muster up much enthusiasm. After all, this audition was supposed to be hers. "I think they just wanted a redhead. That's why they didn't audition you."

"Sure," Dana replied, rising abruptly. "Let's go home."

"You're not mad, are you?" Alison asked as they rode down in the elevator. "I'm really sorry. All I did was sit there."

Dana finally gave her a tremulous smile. "I know. I don't mean to be a wet blanket. It wasn't your fault."

"Oh, Dana, it really wasn't," Alison replied with relief. She hated it when people got mad at her. "In fact, if anything, I feel like I got swept up in a tornado."

Dana's grin was more genuine now. "Besides, if I can't be a star, it's cool that my best friend is one."

"I'm not a star, Dana. I don't even know if I can do the part," Alison replied helplessly. Suddenly, the enormity of what had happened hit her—and it felt like a steel ball crashing into her stomach.

"Well, you're right, maybe you can't."

"Dana!"

"How many times have you told me you hate being the center of attention? What makes you think you want to be on television?"

"Good question," Alison said, sighing. "Maybe I did get caught up in Mr. Greenspan's enthusiasm. But when he started talking to me, I started to feel like I really could do it."

The girls found Dana's car and took off. "Let's face it," Alison continued, "this is the opportunity of a lifetime."

"You've got that right. You've got to give it a shot."

Alison paused. "What am I talking about? I don't even know if my parents will let me take the part."

"Sure they will. A chance to be a TV star? Whose parents wouldn't?"

"Mine," Alison said grimly.

Dana thought about it for a few seconds. "Yeah, could be. Your parents are pretty strict. How are you going to break it to them?"

"I haven't the faintest idea."

Alison sat back and tried to imagine how her parents would react to her incredible news. *Badly* was the word that came to mind.

Maybe she should tell her mother first. Her mom was pretty cool. When she had first told her mother about Dana going out for auditions, Mrs. Blake had said, "I hope Dana knows what she's getting into. Still, it is kind of exciting."

"Mom," Alison had replied, "I never thought I'd hear you say something like that."

"Why not?" Her mother seemed surprised.

"I didn't think you'd want *me* running off for interviews."

"Well, it isn't what you're interested in doing, Alison. I hope I would support you if you felt you had some kind of talent. Dana's really taking her destiny into her own hands. I admire that."

Would her mother be quite so admiring if it was Alison who was grabbing at a career? One thing she knew for sure: Her dad wouldn't.

To her father especially, Alison was still a little girl, someone to be protected. He hated anything that smacked of her growing up. She remembered all too clearly the terrible fuss he had made when she first started dating. Why, he hadn't even wanted her to go to overnight camp when she was a kid. Alison had learned over the years that fighting him on every issue just didn't work, so she chose her battles carefully. It was pretty much a given that announcing she was leaving school to take a role on a situation comedy was going to set off the mother of all battles. Thinking about it, Alison's expression became one of steely determination. Well, this was one battle she was fixing to win. She'd never felt so adamant about anything before. But then, she'd never had such a tremendous opportunity land in her lap before, either.

"Hello, Ali," Dana said, taking a hand off the steering wheel to wave it in front of Alison's face. "Come back to earth with the rest of us noncelebrities."

"I was just trying to figure out what to tell my mother. And my father."

"Yeah, *he's* not going to be too happy. He still wants you to be a lawyer like him, right?"

Ali could feel all her new-found determination oozing out of her. "Uh-huh."

Mr. Blake had a very successful law practice, much

of it entertainment law. Just last week, for about the five zillionth time, he'd said, "You can join my firm, Ali. Blake and Blake, attorneys at law. I can see it now."

"I can't," Ali had muttered, daringly rebellious.

"Don't be so negative," Mr. Blake replied, a bit sharply. "You're a bright girl. There's no reason you can't be a lawyer."

Except that I don't want to, Alison had answered silently.

"Just tell him it's in the stars for you to become an actress," Dana advised. "It was practically fate that got you discovered today. Tell him if you can't take the job, you'll die," she finished dramatically.

Alison laughed. "He could just tell me that being an actress is a fate worse than death. Aside from wanting me to be a lawyer like him, my dad's not too keen on acting as a profession, you know," Alison said with a small sigh.

Dana pulled into Alison's driveway. "Well, the moment of truth is at hand."

"Want me to come in with you? You know, help you explain things?" Dana asked hopefully. Dana loved to be in on everything.

"Uh, thanks," Alison told her, "but I think I better handle this myself."

"Okay, okay, I get the picture," Dana grumbled good-naturedly. "But call me as soon as you know *anything*!"

"I will," Alison promised, as she jumped out of the car.

California was full of gorgeous houses, but Alison always secretly thought hers was one of the nicest, at least in their Westwood neighborhood. The long, sprawling brick house with its stained-glass windows was surrounded by flowers bursting with color. Although Mrs. Blake liked to dabble in the garden, it was really the gardeners who neatly trimmed the lawn and the shrubs and who decided where the pink sprays of flowers would mix with the white and red.

But Alison didn't have time to admire the flowers today. She knew she'd better get inside. It was pretty late.

Sure enough, Mrs. Blake appeared as soon as Alison dropped her purse on the hall table. "Alison! I was beginning to worry, honey. Where on earth were you?"

"Didn't you get my phone message?"

"Well, you said you were going to be late, but . . ." Mrs. Blake glanced at her watch. "It's almost eight."

"Is Dad home?" Alison asked.

"Yes, he's in the living room. We've already eaten, but there's plenty of leftovers. Can I fix you a plate?"

"I'm not hungry. I need to talk to you both. Right away."

A concerned expression crossed Mrs. Blake's face, a face that looked remarkably like her daughter's. "Alison, you look so serious. What's wrong?"

"Nothing." Alison tried to smile, but her face felt

stiff and unnatural. "Actually, something terrific has happened."

"Terrific?"

"Let's go see Dad. I want to tell you both together."

Her father was reading the newspaper. Tall, with an athletic build kept in shape by tennis and golf, Mr. Blake seemed younger than a lot of the dads. Only his hair, thinning on the top and graying at the sides, gave away his age.

He put down his paper and smiled as he saw Alison. "Hi, hon. Your mother was starting to worry."

"I know," Alison said, sitting across from him on the pink brocade love seat. Mrs. Blake joined her.

"Alison has to talk to us," Mrs. Blake informed her husband. "Something important. And terrific."

Mr. Blake raised his eyebrows. "Oh?"

"Uh, yes. Great news."

Her father wasn't a lawyer for nothing. He knew evidence when he saw it. Alison was sure that her sweaty palms and nervous expression were already giving her away. Better to just say it.

Alison cleared her throat and crossed her fingers. "I got a role in a television show today."

Her parents couldn't have looked more surprised if she had just announced she was offered the starting quarterback spot on the Los Angeles Rams. For a moment or two, they simply goggled at her, speechless.

"But I thought it was Dana . . ." her mother began, finally finding her voice.

"It was supposed to be. I just went to keep her company." Then she launched into her incredible story. She tried to gauge her parents' reactions as she told them about Mr. Greenspan singling her out and then giving her a video test. Mostly they just looked amazed. Her father didn't even interrupt once. Had she ever seen him at a complete loss for words? She couldn't remember it if she had.

Finally, there was nothing else to say. It was their turn.

"Well, Alison, do you want to do it?" her mother asked reasonably.

Before Alison could open her mouth to answer, her dad roared, "What difference does that make, Clare? *I* don't want *my daughter* going into *television*!"

"But, Peter, it isn't every day . . ."

"Are you forgetting I know this business? It's brutal."

"It's so exciting, though. It could be such a wonderful opportunity for Alison."

"Exciting? Wonderful? It's terrifying. I see people—every day—who've had their hearts broken by show business. And worse. Believe me, much worse," he said grimly.

Alison felt her stomach tense. Were they just going to discuss this as if she wasn't even there?

Alison finally found the courage to speak up. "Don't I get to say anything?"

Her parents turned to her, almost surprised, as if they had momentarily forgotten she was there.

"Well, of course you do, sweetheart," her mother said gently.

"I really want to do this."

Mr. Blake threw up his hands. "You *think* you do. It sounds glamorous, I know. But are you prepared to give up your whole life for a television career? Have you thought about that? You'll be stuck on some soundstage while your friends are having fun, going to dances, living a normal life."

"I'll still be able to go to dances with Brad," Alison said in a small voice. "I could still have a normal life."

"And what about school?" Mr. Blake continued, warming to his subject. "How do you expect to get into a top university, and then into law school, if you're being tutored on a set in the middle of a thousand distractions?"

Alison didn't bother to mention she wasn't interested in law school. But she did say, "Jodie Foster went to Yale. And she's been in the movies since she was a little kid." She was glad she remembered that fact. That was something, wasn't it?

Her father wasn't swayed by her argument, though. "Jodie Foster is *one* actress who got an education. I can name you a hundred who didn't."

"Dad, I'll go to college, I promise. Think of the money I'll make. I'll probably be able to pay my own tuition."

"I don't need you to pay tuition, Ali. That's one reason I work hard."

Alison tried to muster more arguments, but they all

seemed to get tangled in her brain. What was the point of trying to explain how she felt, anyway? As always, her father seemed to easily come up with arguments that countered anything she had to say.

"Ali, baby." Her father smiled tenderly at her. "Any kid would want to be on a TV show, but that's what I'm here for. I'm not going to let you make any mistakes."

A small spark of resistance brightened in Alison. "Dad, people have to make their *own* mistakes."

For a second, her father looked taken aback. "Well, sure, but not big ones like this."

"It could turn out to be a wonderful experience." Alison could hear her voice rising. "You're both always trying to protect me. Especially you, Dad. You make me feel like I can't do anything."

Her father stared at her. "What do you mean by that?"

"Dad, you call me Alison Wonderland. You think I'm some wide-eyed kid who's so naive she has to be protected from life. Lots of parents have to worry about their children drinking, or acting wild, or doing drugs. I don't do any of that. All I want to do is be on a television show."

Angry tears formed in Alison's eyes. Winning this part was like a fairy godmother touching her with a wand. It made her feel special in a way nothing else ever had. How could she make her parents understand she couldn't give up the magic?

Mrs. Blake leaned over and gave her daughter a hug.

"I'm sorry, sweetheart. Your father just doesn't think this is a good idea."

Alison pulled away. "What do *you* think? You always just agree with Dad."

"Oh, that's not true," her mother protested.

"Then what do you think? Wouldn't you want to do it if you had the chance?"

Mrs. Blake glanced quickly at her husband, and then back at Alison. "I won't lie to you, Ali. Sure, I would. But that still wouldn't mean it was the right decision."

Estelle, the Blakes' housekeeper, came into the dining room. "There's a visitor for you, Mr. Blake. A Mr. Greenspan."

Ali clapped a hand to her mouth. "Oh, I forgot. Mr. Greenspan, the producer of the show, said he was going to come over tonight to talk about hiring me."

"Dan Greenspan?"

"I *think* his first name is Dan."

"Do you know him, Peter?" Mrs. Blake inquired.

Mr. Blake's face softened. "Yes, from way back. He was one of my first clients, as a matter of fact. He moved to New York about ten years ago and I haven't seen him since, but he's a very talented guy."

Alison hardly dared to let herself hope, but it certainly couldn't hurt that her father liked Dan Greenspan.

"Estelle, send him in," Mr. Blake instructed. He turned to Alison and her mother. "I guess it's only polite to say hello," he said.

It was a hearty hello. Mr. Greenspan gave Mr. Blake a big bear hug, while he expressed surprise that Mr. Blake was Alison's father. Then he greeted Mrs. Blake and Alison.

"Have a seat, Dan," Mrs. Blake invited.

"I guess you've heard your daughter's big news. I said I would explain it, but she wanted to tell you herself."

"It was a surprise, all right," Mr. Blake said dryly.

"You've got to see her on tape, Peter, she's really something."

"I'm sure she is, but as I was just telling Ali, I don't think dropping out of school for a television show is a very good idea."

That was the beginning. Alison knew that her father was good at making a case, but Dan Greenspan seemed just as able. He assured her father that the tutors on the set would be of the highest quality, that he would personally make sure Ali wasn't overworked and had plenty of time for learning and fun. "It's a dream come true for any kid, Peter. Would you deny her this opportunity?" he asked.

Ali kept quiet, but her mother, though she never came right out and said it, made comments that seemed to support Mr. Greenspan's arguments. She asked about the salary, which seemed unbelievably high to Alison, and she wanted to know how many hours Alison would have to work in a day.

"About as many as she'd spend in school, though she might start earlier. The show's going on as a summer replacement—that's why we're starting up so late in the spring. If it takes off, there's a long hiatus that starts around March, and she'd be off for a couple of weeks around Christmas. Of course, school's almost over now, so that would simplify things."

"What if she didn't like it?" Mr. Blake asked.

"Hey, Peter," Mr. Greenspan responded with a laugh, "you're the lawyer. I assume you'll write a contract for Alison that will have all sorts of escape clauses."

"If I write a contract," Mr. Blake corrected.

"You know I'd be the last guy to try and push anything. Heck, I couldn't push you, Peter, even if I tried. But I think it would be a mistake *not* to give Alison this terrific chance. Think about it and let me know what you all decide."

Alison felt like her last hope was walking out the door with Mr. Greenspan. Her dad had been nice to him—they were old friends, after all. But nothing she had seen made her think Mr. Greenspan had changed her father's stubborn mind.

"Let's not talk about it anymore tonight, Ali," her father said, after they had said their good-nights to Mr. Greenspan.

Alison didn't know when she had been more exhausted. "Okay." She thought she would go upstairs and fall asleep before she could even get herself undressed. She was too tired even to call Dana. But to her surprise, sleep didn't come easily at all. Finally, she got up to go downstairs and find herself a nice, boring book. She heard her parents talking in their bedroom, and even though she knew it was wrong, she crept up to the door and listened to what they were saying.

"You know, Peter, it just might be good for her."

"You've said that, Clare, but what do you mean?"

"Ali was right. She has been protected by us. Overprotected in some ways."

"What's wrong with that?" Mr. Blake bristled.

"She's like a little girl. Shy. Not very confident. Why, she never stands up for herself. Dana and Brad practically run her life."

Out in the hallway, Alison frowned. She wouldn't exactly say that.

"So, your way, producers and directors would be running her life."

"I think it would give her a chance to stand on her own."

Alison could hear her father pacing the floor. "You know these child stars can get into all sorts of trouble."

"She's not a child, Peter. I would hope that we've given her enough of a foundation so that wouldn't happen."

Alison would have loved to hear more, but she was afraid her parents might discover her. She snuck back to bed and pulled the covers up tight. It was a warm night, but she was shivering inside. It sounded as if her father were actually wavering. Could the combined arguments of Mr. Greenspan and her mother actually be making a dent? She fell asleep wondering. And hopeful.

Chapter 4

The sun streaming through her window forced Alison to open her eyes. For a moment, Alison only wanted to close them again. Then it all came back to her.

Had her parents made their decision yet? She threw off the covers, threw on some clothes, and hurried downstairs. She found her father alone on the patio sipping his coffee.

"Hi, Dad," she said hesitantly.

"Come over here and give your old dad a kiss."

Alison kissed him on the cheek and then slid into the chair across from him.

"I didn't sleep much last night," he confessed.

"I had weird dreams."

"Were they giving you an Academy Award?" he joked weakly.

"No. I kept wandering through crowds of people, and they all stared at me."

"Well, Ali, that's something you have to consider.

Could you handle everything that would come with fame?"

"I'd sure like to try."

Her father sipped his coffee.

Alison couldn't wait anymore. She was dying to ask the question. "Are you going to let me take the part?"

Mr. Blake sighed. "I'm considering it."

"All right!" Alison couldn't hide her glee.

"Considering it," her father emphasized.

Alison tried to collect her thoughts. Maybe if she said it right, she could make her father understand. "Dad, this is the most amazing thing that ever happened to me. To anyone, maybe. It's the kind of thing every girl dreams about. Please, let me do it."

Her dad sighed. "Look, I know this seems pretty clear-cut to you, but I wouldn't be doing my job as a parent if I didn't investigate it more. Maybe talk to Dan again. Okay?"

She wanted to plead, promise she'd go to law school, anything, but all she said, swallowing hard, was, "Okay."

Saturday dragged endlessly. Dana must have been on the phone spreading the news at dawn, because all sorts of kids called, even ones she didn't know very well. Dana herself called three times before noon, wanting to know if there was anything to report.

"For the third time, Dana, I'll call you when I hear something."

"Did you tell your dad how broadening an experience like this would be?"

"I think that's what he's worrying about," Alison informed her.

The funniest call came from her friend Steve Kaye.

"Hey, Ali, I hear Madonna's really worried," he said.

"Why's that?"

"Because you're going to be America's next superstar."

"Oh, right," she laughed. It was the first time she had laughed since yesterday.

"Maybe you don't quite have all her assets, if you know what I mean . . ."

"Steve!"

"But you're going to have every guy in America after you."

She immediately thought of Brad. He was out of town for the weekend with his parents. She wondered what his response would be when *he* heard the news.

By the time Brad returned on Sunday night, Alison had finally gotten an answer out of her father. It had come with a whimper, not a bang. At breakfast on Sunday morning, he'd said, "I don't want to keep you in suspense any longer, Alison. You can take the part."

"I can?" Alison had squealed. She had jumped up and given both her mother and father quick hugs.

"*But*—and I'm not kidding, Alison—if this doesn't seem like it's working out, for any reason, you are off the show. Dan Greenspan was right, I can find loopholes in contracts with the best of them."

"It'll work out, Dad." *It's got to,* she thought.

Alison dashed to the phone to call Dana. She couldn't stop screaming when Alison told her it was a go.

"Yes! Yes! Alison, this is the best."

"Really? You didn't seem so sure the other day."

"But, Ali, I've realized something since then."

"What's that?"

"Once you're on the show, you can get a job for me!"

Alison felt her stomach tighten. "I just can't go in there and ask them to hire you, Dana."

"Oh, not right away. I wouldn't expect that. But eventually, it will be easy."

"Oh, Dana . . ."

"Don't worry about it right now," Dana said cheerily. "Let's figure out what you're going to wear your first day on the set."

Alison was glad to change the subject. But she got nervous all over again when Brad's name came up.

"How do you think he's going to take it?" Dana asked.

"He'll be excited for me," Alison said, biting her nail.

"He's the jealous type, Alison, you know that."

"There's nothing to be jealous about."

"Right," Dana hooted. "You're going to be on the set with handsome actors and hunky stagehands. Brad won't think a thing of it."

She had to wait until dinnertime to see Brad. She had spent much of the day going over details of her new life with her parents. Dan Greenspan wasn't exactly sure when Alison would be needed for her first day of work, but costume fittings would start very soon. The school would have to be informed, of course. Her father wanted to write down where she was in all her classes, so that her tutor would be sure to know what she was studying. They called her grandmother and a couple of other relatives. Mrs. Blake didn't want them to hear the news from anyone but them. *When does the glamour start?* Alison wondered as she slogged her way through all the practical stuff.

Alison had almost forgotten about Brad until he called right before dinnertime and asked if she could go out for a burger at their favorite drive-in, The Bun. A giant hamburger sat on top of the drive-in, and waiters and waitresses on roller skates came out to the car to take orders.

Alison wanted to blurt out everything over the phone, but she restrained herself. This was news that was better given in person. "Sure, that will be great."

"I really missed you," Brad said softly.

"You were only gone a couple of days."

"Long enough."

"I'll be ready in a half hour. I've got a lot to tell you, Brad."

"Sounds mysterious. See you soon."

Alison was waiting out on the driveway when Brad drove up. As usual, her heart gave a little thump when she saw him. What exactly did it to her? Was it his dark eyes that really never gave away his true emotions, or his muscular body that he spent so much time working on? No, it was the air of daring that radiated off him like heat on a summer day. Alison knew that was a quality lacking in herself. Until now, maybe.

"Hi, babe," Brad said as Alison got into the car. He gave her a small kiss on the cheek. "What did I miss while I was gone?"

Alison cleared her throat. "Well, a lot actually."

As they sped down Santa Monica Boulevard, Alison told her story. Brad could barely keep his eyes on the road. He kept turning around to stare at her.

"Don't do that, Brad. Watch the road." He was driving worse than Dana tonight.

"I've got to make sure you're not jiving me."

"Brad, it's all true."

"Yeah, I guess it is." He didn't sound too happy about it.

He pulled into the drive-in with a squeal of his wheels and stopped so hard that Alison jerked back against her seat. "I can't believe your dad said yes."

"Me either."

"This is one lousy idea," Brad scowled.

Alison couldn't believe it. This was the greatest thing that ever happened to her, and Brad was being a total grinch. "Can't you be happy for me?"

"It is a good break, I guess," he muttered. "For you, if not for me."

Alison softened a little. She wanted to run her hand through Brad's soft, dark hair. He was worried about their relationship. That was kind of sweet. "Brad, this won't make any difference between us."

"Yeah, with all those guys hanging around you?"

"Thanks, but I don't think there will be all that many."

"You won't be able to handle them. Or all the attention either."

"Brad, I'm not some kind of a baby." *Even though everyone thinks I am,* she added silently.

"I guess you'll be gone all day, huh?" Brad said stonily.

"But not all night. Mr. Greenspan even said I'd probably be home in the afternoon at the same time I am now."

"Great, I'll make an appointment between four and five."

"Brad, I thought you of all people would see how important this is. It's pretty exciting stuff, after all."

"I know, I know." Brad said more softly, as he took her hand. "I'm sorry, babe, but this just came out of the blue. I have to get used to it."

Alison smiled weakly at him. "Who knows how long it will last, anyway? Maybe the show will be a big flop and get canceled after a week."

"When do you start?" Brad asked glumly.

"I have costume fittings and stuff right away, but Mr. Greenspan said I *might* be able to finish out the school year with the rest of you guys."

"That's something."

"Oh, Brad, can't we look at this as an adventure?"

"I guess I have to. It's all been decided anyway."

"Everything's going to be the same, I told you."

He looked at her and shook his head. "No, it isn't. Nothing's going to be the same."

When she went to bed that night, Alison wondered if it was going to be another night of tossing and turning. There was so much happening, and her new career hadn't even started yet. She finally felt her eyes growing heavy. *Some weekend,* she thought, for about the thousandth time. She wanted to fall asleep thinking about winning the Emmy, but it was Brad's face she saw before she dozed off. He was mouthing the words, "Nothing will ever be the same again."

Chapter 5

Jamie walked out into the bright sunshine, a smile on her face. *Good-bye, Ralph's Market,* she thought happily. She stuffed her last paycheck into her purse. The job had paid pretty well—if you counted overtime—and her coworkers were nice, but she was certainly glad to have rung up her last bag of carrots.

Since Mr. Greenspan had called her a week ago and told her she had the job, she could feel her life changing more every day. Her mother and her agent, Meg, had been absolutely delirious when she had gotten the news and, of course, so had she. Jamie still didn't know how she had waited the two whole days it took Mr. Greenspan to call after the audition.

"Jamie," he had said, after greeting her heartily. "I've got great news."

Jamie's heart had leapt. "I've got the part?"

"You're our Wendy," he agreed.

"Oh, thank you," she cried.

"You're entirely welcome, Jamie. We're happy to have you aboard."

Trying to catch her breath, Jamie said, "I was sure you had picked someone else."

"I'm sorry it took so long, but I had to make a quick trip out of town. Besides, by waiting, one more role fell into place."

"Oh?"

"I don't know if you noticed her, but there was this lovely girl in the waiting room. She had red hair too."

"Yes, I saw her." *She and her snippy friend were gossiping about me,* Jamie added silently.

"I had the idea that to have two redheads on the show would make your rivalry even more fun. Alison Blake's her name."

"So she got the part."

Mr. Greenspan chuckled. "Yes, but I had a terrible time getting her signed."

"Oh?" Jamie said carefully. She knew how important it was to keep cool, even though she was dying to hear more. After all, anyone at an audition wanted a part, right?

"Well, this girl was only there with her friend, she didn't want to audition. Alison was perfect for the part, she tested beautifully. But her parents are very protective of Alison, and they don't need the money. I had to do a lot of fast talking to get them to agree to let her on the show."

As she walked home from the market, Jamie could feel her mood grow grim. She thought, as she had thought so many times since that phone call, *How could Mr. Greenspan have hired an amateur for the role?* There were so many qualified actresses around. Jamie thought about how long she herself had been out of acting work. What if this Alison hadn't taken the role? Did that mean Mr. Greenspan would have chosen someone else for *her* role? That horrible thought had crossed her mind during the call, but she had been afraid to bring it up.

And if she was being honest, something else was bugging her. She couldn't help feeling a little jealous of this rich kid whose mommy and daddy were so protective that they didn't want their darling little girl to be in a television show. Quite a change from her mother, who had danced around the room with Jamie's four-year-old sister Elsie in her arms when she heard that Jamie had gotten the role.

"Do you think I should quit my job?" Mrs. O'Leary had asked when she finally put Elsie down.

Jamie had been startled. She knew that her mother's job as a waitress at the Tick Tock restaurant wasn't the greatest in the world, but she hadn't thought about her mother actually quitting. Jamie would be making a good salary on the show. Still, she wasn't ready to be the sole support of their family quite yet.

"Mom, you know how weird show business can be," Jamie said carefully. "Who knows how long *Sticks and Stones* will be on the air? It could be canceled after a couple of weeks. Maybe we should play it safe for now."

Trying to catch her breath, Mrs. O'Leary flopped down on the couch. "I suppose you're right. And I've got health insurance at the restaurant. That counts for something. But maybe we could use some of your money to put Elsie into a better day care. I don't know how well that Mrs. Grant takes care of the kids who go to her house. Sometimes I wonder."

"That's a good idea."

Mrs. O'Leary looked around. "And maybe we could get out of here, find a better apartment."

That was one of Jamie's dreams, too. She had had a lot of dreams since she had left *The Happydale Girls,* but none of them had ever come true. She hoped this one would. "Soon, Mom."

"My little girl back on top, where she belongs." Mrs. O'Leary's expression was one Jamie seldom saw—happy, proud, and satisfied. "Everything's going to be wonderful again, just like the old days."

"It wasn't all perfect," Jamie murmured. She tried not to think about it, but there were some bad things about being a child star. It was exhausting, for one, and it was often confusing to have people fawn over her. The worst thing, though, was having the show end and being left out in the cold.

But Mrs. O'Leary had looked at Jamie indignantly. "What are you talking about? You were famous. We were living in our own home." She looked around the apartment. "Not some three-roomer over a Chinese restaurant." Lowering her voice, she added, "Your dad was with us."

Jamie didn't know why her mother was always so nostalgic whenever Jack O'Leary's name came up. Sometimes Jamie thought she remembered him better than her mom did, even though she had only been a kid when he left. If he was so great, where had he been the past few years? Not helping them, that was for sure.

As she walked along the down-at-its-heels street that she lived on, Jamie pushed her father out of her mind. Why think about him when there were actually some good things happening in her life?

She climbed up the stairs to the apartment, through the hallways reeking of various Chinese spices, their smells all mingled together. She used to like Chinese food.

As soon as she walked into the apartment, Elsie jumped up from the TV to run and give her a kiss.

"Hi, sweetie," Jamie said, swinging her sister around. "You're not dressed yet."

Jamie was using part of her last paycheck to take her mother, Elsie, and Meg, her agent, out to lunch. Then, maybe, she would do a little shopping. She needed a few things to wear to the studio. She didn't want to look like Alison Blake's poor relation.

"Mom's taking a bath first," Elsie informed her. "She says I get the tub too greemy."

"Grimy," Jamie corrected her with a laugh.

Her mother often lamented the fact that Elsie had gotten none of her sister's good looks. Even as a baby, Elsie had been plain.

Sometimes Mrs. O'Leary said, "It's too bad Elsie doesn't look like you did at that age. I'd have her at every talent agency in town."

Jamie hated that comment. "Mom! She'll hear you."

"Oh, she doesn't understand."

If Elsie did, it never seemed to bother her. And as far as Jamie was concerned, Elsie was just about perfect. Who cared if her wren-brown hair hung straight as wet laundry or that she was as skinny as a broom handle? Elsie was kind and funny and sweet.

"My dolls and I are watching television," Elsie told her.

"Okay, you do that. I'll wait 'til Mom is out of the tub, then I'll bathe you."

"I'm done," Mrs. O'Leary said, coming out of the bedroom she shared with Elsie. Jamie slept on the sofa bed in the living room.

"You look nice, Mom."

"Do I?" Mrs. O'Leary asked, pleased.

Jamie was stretching it a little bit, but so what? Even though Mrs. O'Leary was wearing her best dress, it was already several years old and starting to look it. *New clothes for Mom,* Jamie thought. That was something else to put on the top of her list.

Mrs. O'Leary had been so pretty once. Before Jamie was born she had been an extra in the movies. Up on the wall of the living room were her mother's most prized possessions, movie stills taken during the filming of her three movies. In two of them, she was strictly in the background, but in the largest of the three pictures, she was right up at the front of a crowd in a wild pink minidress and white boots, her long red hair hanging down to her shoulders.

Even though it was sometimes boring listening to her mother talk over and over about her days in the movies, Jamie was sure Mrs. O'Leary had been a different person then. She lit up when she talked about those days, and Jamie could catch a glimpse of that carefree young woman.

"Are we meeting Meg at the restaurant?" Mrs. O'Leary asked.

Jamie nodded.

"I certainly hope she manages your career half as good as your father did."

Jamie could feel herself starting to get angry. "Ma, don't rewrite history, please. I'm sure the people at the studio thought he was a big buttinsky. He was always trying to get them to give me a bigger part in the show or add some perk like decorating my dressing room. None of the other parents did those kinds of things."

"Those other parents were'nt their kids' managers. Why, if it hadn't been for him, you wouldn't have had a career at all."

"Just because he sent my picture into some contest—

"Where a talent agent saw it," Mrs. O'Leary interrupted. "I remember him saying the day he put that photo of you in the envelope . . ."

"My little girl will win this thing hands down,"

Jamie finished for her. She had heard the story enough times to know how it ended. "Just 'cause he was right about that doesn't make him right about everything. Where's all that money I made?"

Mrs. O'Leary looked down. "You'll come into some of your money when you're of age."

"That was the money he had to put away by law. The rest of it he just lost with all his brilliant money-making schemes. Too bad he wasn't as good at managing money as he was at managing my career."

"Are you talking about Daddy?" Elsie asked, looking up from the television.

Jamie raised one eyebrow at her mother.

"Is Daddy coming to see us?" Elsie asked.

"I doubt it, kiddo," Jamie replied.

"Well, you never know," Mrs. O'Leary murmured.

"I can't believe you still want to see him."

After Jamie's career had come to a grinding halt, her father had disappeared. When Jamie was working, it was written into her contract that he would get a salary as her manager. That meant when Jamie's job ended, so did his. For a while, he had tried his hand at different jobs, managing a rock group that made up in volume what it lacked in talent. Later, after the group broke up, he sold insurance. Then there were other jobs, too many to remember. Mr. O'Leary couldn't make a go of any of them.

By that time, they had moved out of their house to save money and were living in an apartment, one that was nicer than their current place. One day, he had told Mrs. O'Leary he was going to look for a job down in San Diego. He had driven off in the car, and they hadn't seen him for another year. He had come back briefly, all apologies and flowers for her mother, stuffed animals for her, and stayed a few months. But when Mrs. O'Leary had learned she was pregnant with Elsie, Mr. O'Leary had thrown up his hands and said they couldn't afford another child. Within a few weeks, he had taken off again.

Since then he had come back a couple of times for short visits. Elsie was delighted when her father turned up. Jamie figured Elsie thought of him kind of like Santa, who showed up with toys and kisses and easy promises. Her mother always welcomed him, a little wistfully, as if she hoped he would stay. Jamie, on the other hand, hardly said a word to her father. She couldn't stand him for betraying them and abandoning them, and she wanted to make sure that he knew it.

On his last visit, he had tried to talk to her. Sitting on the couch, twisting his hands, he said, "Jamie girl, I know you're mad at me."

Jamie busied herself picking up some of Elsie's toys.

"Jamie, I didn't want to break up the family, but things weren't working out," he said plaintively. "It's been hard, real hard for me lately."

"For you!" she exploded. "Mom and I both have jobs. You hardly ever send us any money. How do you think it's been for us?"

"I just can't seem to get myself situated."

"Well, when you do, and you can take care of your family, let us know." Then she had walked out of the room.

Jamie shook her head. She had hoped today was going to be pleasant. The last person she should be thinking about was Jack O'Leary. But her mother seemed to be reading her thoughts. "You shouldn't be so hostile, Jamie. He is your father after all."

"Some father," she replied with an edge to her voice. "I don't know how you can be so forgiving."

"Why are you fighting?" Elsie asked worriedly.

"We're not, Elsie. Ma, we'd better get going."

Giving Elsie her bath and then getting ready herself calmed Jamie.

"I'm sorry," she apologized as they walked to the car.

"I know," Mrs. O'Leary said softly.

"Things are going to be better now, and I'm going to make sure of that myself."

But she didn't know if she felt secure enough in this job to do it right away. Suddenly, she felt like a lot of responsibility was crashing down on her shoulders. A new apartment, day care for Elsie, clothes for her mother. Could she handle it all? Alison Blake flashed through her mind. No one was going to ask her to kick in to support the family. Rich Miss Blake would probably put her salary away all nice and safe for a rainy day that would probably never come.

———

The lunch was fun. They went to a little Italian place on Melrose Avenue, where Jamie ate more spaghetti carbonara and garlic bread than was probably good for her. Everyone said the camera added ten pounds to your normal weight.

"Look at me make the spageggi snake go in my mouth," Elsie demanded. She slurped a strand through pursed lips.

"Elsie," Mrs. O'Leary said with a frown, "that's bad manners. Especially in public."

"Oh, let her have some fun," Meg Wildman said. "It's not so bad to be the center of attention," she added gently.

If anyone would know, it was Meg. Large, with wild, blonde hair, Meg's fashion rule of thumb seemed to be the splashier the print, the brighter the colors, the better. Today, she was wearing a flowing dress with a green and pink geometric design. "Now I don't want to interrupt the party with business, but I thought this would be a good time to sign your contract." She pulled it out of her enormous leather bag with a flourish. "After all, it *is* why we're celebrating."

"What's that?" Elsie asked, pointing at the contract, almost getting close enough to smear it with marinara sauce.

"It's the answer to a prayer," Mrs. O'Leary murmured.

"It says I'm going to work," Jamie told her sister. Elsie wrinkled her nose. "Work sounds hard."

"Work can be fun, too," Jamie assured her.

"You've read this before, but this is the official document." Meg offered Jamie her gold and pink enamel pen. "Want to sign?"

"I sure do."

Pen poised, Jamie suddenly glanced up at Meg. "What about billing? Where will my name be in the credits?"

Meg looked surprised. "I didn't know you cared about such things."

"Oh, I don't expect my name to appear before the stars', but what about this Alison Blake person, for instance? She's a nobody. I certainly think my name should come before hers."

Meg reached over, took the contract, and scanned it. "Yes, yours will be the first of the kids' names to appear on the screen." She handed the contract back.

"Good," Jamie said. She signed with a flourish, pretending it was an autograph. She could feel the old excitement coursing through her.

While they were having their coffee, Elsie started to get cranky.

"I think she needs a nap," Mrs. O'Leary apologized. "She's not used to all this excitement, eating in a restaurant."

None of us are, Jamie thought. Taking some crumpled bills out of her purse, she picked up the check. Meg grabbed it out of her hand.

"Hey, this was supposed to be my party," Jamie protested.

"No way you're paying this check," Meg replied. "Don't forget, as your agent, I'm making money off this deal, too."

"All right," Jamie said, letting go of the check. She couldn't deny that having a little more money for clothes would be welcome.

"I hoped we could go shopping with you," Mrs. O'Leary said as they walked out the door, her arms full of a sleeping Elsie. "But . . ."

"No, Mom, get Elsie home."

"I have another appointment, or I'd go with you," Meg said.

"It's fine, really. I like to shop on my own. All the shops are in walking distance, and I'll get a bus home."

To tell the truth, Jamie was relieved that she was going alone. Her mother wasn't exactly hip to the latest fashions, and for once, Jamie was determined that she was going to look hot and with it.

And if any teenager wanted to look hot and with it, Melrose Avenue was the place to go. Melrose was a street that ran through Los Angeles, but whenever anyone spoke of Melrose, they meant one strip of it, in West Los Angeles, where dozens of clothing stores crowded against one another. And they didn't sell just any clothes. On Melrose you could get the shortest skirts, the tightest dresses, the coolest leather biker jackets, the hottest colors and patterns, and the ul- tralatest of every kind of fashion. Demure schoolgirl dresses and preppie basics were sold elsewhere.

Jamie used to go to Melrose and window-shop. She would examine the clothes and the displays to see if there was any way to take the great looks she was seeing and adapt them to the meager assortment of clothes in her closet.

Thrift shops helped. Jamie had become a master at finding just the right scarf or belt or bag for a couple of dollars, or a pair of inexpensive earrings that looked like they'd cost more than they actually had. But now, with a good salary only weeks away, Jamie was ready to blow some serious money on Melrose. To get the real thing for once. It felt great.

Saturdays were always crowded on Melrose, and today was no exception. The street was a tourist mecca, too. You could always tell the visitors from the locals, too. The out-of-towners were the ones in nerdy casual clothes and sneakers with cameras hanging around their necks. They were out today, boy. In some places, Jamie had to walk in the street because the sidewalks were so crowded.

She walked into a store called Poopsie's and rummaged through the racks. She had spent all sorts of time wandering around Melrose in the past, dreaming about buying. But now that the moment had come, Jamie wasn't sure what she should be buying for her new career. Actresses didn't shy away from short skirts or flamboyant fabrics, of course, but she didn't want to walk on the set and be the only one dressed up while everyone else wore jeans or something. Grabbing a black crushed velvet dress with skinny straps, and a revealing gold lace bustier and matching metallic skirt, Jamie wondered what sort of clothes Alison wore. The kind that cost a lot, that was for sure.

Jamie took a few more everyday items and walked into the dressing room. So she didn't see Alison and Dana walking through the door of Poopsie's a few minutes behind her.

"I don't know about this, Dana," Alison whispered as she looked around the store. "Melrose is not really my thing."

"Well, it should be," Dana replied stoutly. "Pretty soon everyone in America is going to know who you are. It would be nice if you didn't look like a total dork when they do."

Alison felt her heart start to beat a little faster. She hated it when Dana called her a dork. But even worse was Dana saying everyone in America was going to know her. Not that many kids at her own high school knew her, for pete's sake.

Dana didn't notice Alison's nervousness. She was holding up a wild, neon-green paisley dress. "What do you think of this?"

"It's so short," Alison squeaked.

"No, it isn't. Gosh, Ali," Dana said with exasperation. "Get with the program."

A salesgirl, with a streak of purple down her otherwise straight brown hair, came up to them. "Can I help you?"

Dana's "yes" overpowered Alison's "no."

"Which is it?" the girl asked, bored.

"Alison here is going to be starring on a new television show. She needs some terrific clothes," Dana answered.

"You are? Well, of course you do!" Now the girl's eyes lit with interest. "What's the show?"

"Sticks and Stones," Alison answered, ready to kill Dana.

"Oh, I'll be watching for it. Now, tell me what you need."

"Something she can wear to work. And on interview shows," Dana improvised.

"I know just what you want," the salesgirl said enthusiastically. "One of the soap stars was in here just the other day looking for a dress to wear on *Entertainment Tonight.*"

Alison and Dana trailed the girl around as she picked out a whole armful of items. Alison didn't even get a good look at any of them.

"Try these," the girl said as she showed them to a dressing room.

"Let me see them first," Alison said as the door closed behind the salesgirl.

She inspected one outfit after another. "I'd never wear anything like these."

"You're nuts," Dana replied. "They're way cool. At least try them on."

Reluctantly, Alison stripped out of her flowered sundress and put on a black crushed velvet slinky number that didn't seem too bad until she got a close look at it. "It's so tight," she complained. "It looks like I'm wearing a slip!"

"That's the way it's supposed to be, Ali." Dana sighed enviously. "And you sure have the figure for it."

Alison stared at herself in the mirror. She wondered if her father would even let her out of the house in this dress.

"You look like a model. Or a television star."

"Do you think so?" She had to admit she was starting to like it better.

"Take it," Dana advised.

"All right." Now she was getting into the swing of this shopping business. "Let me see what else we've got there."

There were two catsuits, one in a leopard print, a short purple skirt and matching crop top, and an electric blue gauzy blouse with tiny gold sequin stars all over it that also looked good.

"What about this leather jacket?"

"It's so expensive," Alison fretted.

"Didn't your mother give you her credit card?" Dana asked.

Alison nodded. "She told me to get whatever I needed."

"You need all of this," Dana said decisively.

Excitement fluttered through Alison. "Maybe I do."

Carrying out the load of clothing she had decided to buy, Alison stopped and looked over in the direction of the line where customers were making their purchases. "Look, Dana. Isn't that the girl that we saw in Mr. Greenspan's office? He said she got a part in the show, too."

Dana nodded. "That's her all right. Maybe you should go up to her and say something."

"Oh, I couldn't," Alison replied, shaking her head.

"Why the heck not? You're going to be working together. You're going to be playing stepsisters."

"I guess it would be polite. I wonder if she's as nervous about this whole thing as I am."

"I wouldn't mind meeting her myself," Dana said.

"Okay. She's at the front of the line. Let's catch her as she's about to leave." Alison had so many fears about working on this show. It would be nice to talk to someone who was going through the same thing.

As Jamie headed for the door, Alison, her arms still full of clothes, hurried over to her. "Excuse me," she said. She didn't have a hand free to tap her on the shoulder.

At first Jamie didn't hear her, but at Alison's louder, "Excuse me," she turned around. *Well, well,* she thought. *Look who's here.*

"You don't know me," Alison began hesitantly.

Jamie just stood there, pretending Alison was right, letting her muddle through the awkward introduction.

"My name is Alison Blake, and I'm going to be on *Sticks and Stones* with you. This is my friend Dana Jones."

Jamie glanced at all the clothes Alison held. She was

probably about to charge them all on her parents' credit card. It made the bag in her hand seem awfully light.

"You are Jamie, right?" Alison asked.

"Jamie O'Leary. So *you're* going to be on the show," she said coolly.

"Yes. I'm playing Jane."

There was an awkward silence, then Jamie asked, "So what else have you done?"

"Done?"

"In television. Or in film?"

"Uh, nothing. I've never been in anything before."

Jamie felt a small twinge of satisfaction at the nervous, unhappy look on Alison's face. She'd made her point.

"Well, I'm sure you'll catch on quickly," Jamie said.

"I hope so. It's all going to be so new. Did you have trouble at first?"

Jamie gave a little laugh. "Hey, I've been on television practically all my life. I was too young to be scared when I first started. But, yeah, it can be tough."

"You were a *Happydale* girl, right?" Alison asked. Jamie nodded.

"What was it like?" Dana wanted to know.

"Parts of it were great. Just acting of course is terrific. And all the fame and money that goes with it. But it's also a lot of long hours and sitting around. Difficult people to deal with, too. You've got to be tough." Jamie had a feeling that Alison didn't have a tough bone in her body.

"You're so lucky," Alison sighed. "You know all about this stuff. I bet you're not nervous at all."

"Why should I be?" Jamie wasn't about to let Alison know how many hours she had spent staring at the ceiling instead of sleeping. How uncool.

"No, of course not," Alison murmured.

"Well, I guess I'll see you at the studio," Jamie said, suddenly wanting to get away. Alison's anxiety was contagious. She just wouldn't let herself show her nervousness like Alison did.

"See you." Alison watched Jamie swing out the door.

"Do you think she's going to be fun to work with?" Dana asked as Alison got in line to pay for her clothes.

"I guess." Alison had been feeling nervous enough about her big step into show business. This meeting with Jamie hadn't helped at all.

Dana sensed her feelings. "Hey, don't worry about it. Jamie's been around, sure, but you'll do great. Mr. Greenspan said so."

Alison nodded, but only one thought kept racing around her head. *What if he's wrong?*

Chapter 6

Dana stretched out on the chaise lounge. "This is the life," she said. "You're going to miss not having time to sit out by the pool, Ali."

Alison wondered if Dana was right. Even though she was lucky enough to have a pool in her backyard, she never really took full advantage of it. She always assumed that the pool would be right there waiting for her whenever she had the time. Well, she would still have the pool, but would she have the time?

Alison's friend Pam stuck her head out of the pool. Her normally curly blonde hair lay flat against her head. "Where are the boys?"

Alison shrugged. "They said they'd be here half an hour ago."

Pam got out of the pool and dried herself off. Dana and Alison exchanged glances. Pam had the kind of figure they could only dream about, and her striped bikini really showed it off.

"You better put on a coverup," Dana suggested, "or Elliot will go crazy. To say nothing of Steve."

"No," Pam said, flopping down on chair. "Steve is all yours."

"What am I going to do with that guy?" Dana asked plaintively. "He's asked me out three times this month. I've said no three times. Why doesn't he get the message?"

Alison knew why. Steve had confided in her that he had been reading a book about the power of positive thinking. It said you should set your mind on a goal and then never give up until you had obtained it. Apparently the author of the book had never met Dana.

"Steve is an interesting guy," Pam said. "He's sure a brain. And cute, too."

"And short," Dana replied.

"He's taller than you," Alison pointed out.

"Hey, why is everyone always pushing Steve on me? He's fine for someone else, but I just don't feel *it* when I look at him."

"Well, I can't argue with that," Pam said. "Either you feel *it* or you don't."

How could her friends be so sure about how they felt? Alison wondered. Sometimes she looked at Brad, and her heart melted. She couldn't believe that such a good-looking guy was interested in her. And when he kissed her, well, she melted even more. But often she felt as if Brad thought of her as some pretty little doll he could pick up and play with when he was in the mood and ignore when he wasn't. He wasn't happy about her new career, that she knew. He had taken her to calling her Sarah, short for Sarah Bernhardt, the famous actress, and even though he said it jokingly, Alison didn't think it was all that funny.

Sometimes Alison couldn't believe his extreme lack of interest in the TV show. She was going in for her first costume fitting in a couple of days, and she was really excited. But whenever Alison wanted to talk about the show, Brad always changed the subject. Alison sighed. Her life had become so nerve-racking. She didn't know what her new world was going to be like, and her old world was changing, too.

More than once, more than a hundred times actually, Alison had wondered if she had made a mistake by saying yes to this job. But she was darned if she was going to give it up before at least making a stab at it. She couldn't seem to forget Jamie's remarks. She had never done this before. Would she stick out like a sore thumb when the show went into rehearsal? If only she had someone to talk things over with. Dana, who was dying to have a chance like this, couldn't understand her ambivalence at all, while her parents, especially her dad, would be more than eager to have her forget the whole thing.

She was roused out of her thoughts by the sound of male voices. Brad, Steve, and Elliot were heading toward them, laughing and horsing around.

"Hi, you guys," Pam said, shading her eyes. "Where have you been?"

"Looking at cars," Elliot replied.

"Who's getting a car?" Dana wanted to know.

Steve smiled at her. "Me. I turned sixteen last month, in case you forgot."

"He's looking at Corvettes," Elliot said. "Can you believe his dad would plunk down that kind of cash?"

Dana looked at Steve with more interest than she had ever shown before. "Really?"

"He said I could get a sports car. He had a good year in the stock market," Steve said, clearly a little embarrassed.

"But still . . ."

"I probably won't get anything that expensive." Steve laughed self-consciously. "I'd hate to crack it up."

"You wouldn't," Alison said seriously. "You're probably going to be the safest driver of all of us."

"Yeah, Dudley Doright," Brad said mockingly. "Mr. All A Student. You're always trying to make the rest of us look bad."

"That's not too difficult in your case," Pam said dryly.

Brad picked up her towel and tried to swat her with it.

"Hey, quit it," she squealed, grabbing it away from him.

"Any more comments out of you," Brad warned, "and you get thrown in the pool."

"By you and what army?" Pam scoffed.

"I'll help," Elliot offered.

"Uh-uh, I can handle this one all on my own," Brad smirked.

"Settle down, Brad dear," Pam said with a cool smile. "If you get all overheated, you'll wind up with a stroke."

Laughing, Brad pulled up a deck chair next to Pam's. *He hasn't even said hello to me,* Alison thought.

They talked about school and the upcoming prom. Brad, Elliot, and Steve were all juniors, and Elliot was on the prom committee. He assured the group that this dance was going to be the flashiest that Madison High had ever seen. Alison had just assumed that she and Brad would be going, but he hadn't actually asked her. The way he was looking at Pam, Alison wondered if he had another date in mind.

"You should be working on the TV show by then, right, Ali?" Steve asked.

"I think so," Alison said uncertainly. "Who knows what my schedule will be like? It seems to change all the time."

"The drudgery of a television star's life," Brad said sarcastically.

"That's not what I meant, Brad."

"Of course it isn't," Dana added loyally. She shot a frown in Brad's direction.

"I think you ought to have a party," Steve suggested. "You know, a farewell to Madison High."

Alison looked surprised. She had never had a party at her house. There was no particular reason why she hadn't. Parties just always seemed to her like things you went to other kids' houses for.

Pam clapped her hands. "That would be great! This place is so gorgeous, too. It could be the best party of the year."

"Gee, I don't know," Alison said. "I'm not sure what my mother would say."

"She's right over there in the garden," Dana noted. "Why don't we call her over and ask her?"

Before Alison could reply, the kids were calling out to Mrs. Blake. She pushed back her straw gardening hat, waved, and walked over to them.

"What's up?" she asked.

"We think Ali should have a party before she wanders off into the wonderful world of show business," Dana said.

"Well, I hope *wandering off* isn't the right term, but that sounds like a fun idea."

"Can it be a splash party?" Pam asked.

"I don't think so, Pam. We'd have to hire a lifeguard and all. Wouldn't it be more fun to just get dressed up?"

"Sure," Pam said. "I'm easy."

"All right! It's happening," Brad said.

Nobody asked me what I want, Alison thought. Did she actually want to be the hostess of some big bash?

"Of course, my husband or I or both of us would have to be home."

None of the kids said anything, but Elliot made a face.

"I saw that, Elliot," Mrs. Blake said, with a smile. "I won't take it personally."

"Didn't mean it personally," Elliot mumbled, embarrassed.

"Why don't you kick around a date and let me know when you'd like to have it. Then we'll start making the arrangements."

"Your mom's okay," Elliot said, once Mrs. Blake was out of earshot, "even if she does think she needs to chaperon us."

Steve grinned. "Face it, Elliot, she does."

Brad glanced over at Alison. "You don't look very happy about this shindig."

"Yeah, I am," Alison said, trying desperately to convince herself she wasn't lying. "I'm just not sure who I'd invite . . ."

"We are," Pam and Dana chorused.

"Then I guess I'll get plenty of help with the guest list."

"Count on it," Pam assured her.

Alison shrugged. "What the heck? Let's party."

"You're sure I look all right?" Alison asked her mother for the tenth time. She was on her way to the costume fitting.

"Yes," Mrs. Blake said patiently.

"It's a new look for me." Alison had paired the blouse with the stars that she had bought at Poopsie's with a short black skirt and gold belt. She had no idea what someone wore to a costume fitting, but assumed that if anyone would know if she looked dumb, it would be the show's designer.

"You look very sweet and very pretty," her mother told her.

"Sweet! You think I look sweet?" a horrified Alison cried. "That's it. I'm changing."

"No, no," Mrs. Blake backtracked. "Not sweet like sugary. Just nice."

"I'm supposed to look trendy."

"But you're also supposed to be the nice girl on this show, so you don't want to look like a punk, either."

Alison made a face. "No one wants to look like a punk anymore."

"Excuse me. Perhaps I'm a bit behind the times."

Alison sat down next to her mother on the bed. "I wish you were driving me to the studio."

"Alison! You don't want to go in the limousine?"

"I'll feel weird."

"Why, most kids would adore it. I think it was nice of Mr. Greenspan to send it for you."

"It just seems unreal for me to be riding around in a limo. I thought I knew how much my life was going to change," Alison said, in a troubled voice, "but I'm starting to realize I didn't have a clue."

Her mother looked at her searchingly. "Alison, do you want to forget about this television show? It's not too late, you know. Your father wrote your contract with plenty of escape clauses, and one of them is that you can leave anytime before the show actually goes into production."

Alison felt like a little girl, afraid of the dark again, ready to cry out for someone to save her from unseen monsters. Sure, she wished she could say, "Help! Get me out of this!" but she was determined to stick with her decision. Besides, there was still a part of her, even if it had now shrunk to a rather tiny part, that said, "This might be fun."

"No, I want to do it," she answered, trying to sound firm and sure.

"Well, I guess you should give it a shot now that you've gone this far," her mother agreed. Mrs. Blake patted her daughter's knee. "You've just got the jitters."

Could the jitters be terminal? Alison asked herself. She stood up as she saw a big blue limousine pull into the driveway. "It's here. I better hurry and get my stuff."

Waiting downstairs in the car, looking around her with a mixture of delight and envy, was Jamie O'Leary. She had been absolutely thrilled when she learned that a limo was picking her up, even though she had worried a little that the car would look radically out of place in her neighborhood.

She was right. The limo took up practically the whole street, and passersby stopped to look. Even though it embarrassed her, Jamie let her mother and Elsie come down and take a peek inside. The bored driver didn't even turn around as the duo *ooh*ed and *aah*ed.

"A little television. There's a little television in the car!" Elsie exclaimed.

"And a bar," her mother said.

"Don't worry, Mom. All I'll have is soda," Jamie kidded her.

"I wouldn't worry about such a thing," Mrs. O'Leary said indignantly.

Now, as Jamie sat waiting in the car, she thought maybe she would have something to drink. Her head thrown back against the creamy leather upholstery, a sparkling soda poured into one of the cut-crystal wine glasses . . . Now that would make a cool, collected picture when Alison finally arrived. But no, Jamie decided, the drink would be too much trouble. Besides, she wanted to look more closely at the house.

Would the Blakes think it was odd that she was wandering around outside their house? Oh heck, she could always say she was just stretching her legs. Getting out of the car, Jamie walked up the driveway. Flowers in bright profusion bordered the asphalt driveway, and their perfume filled the air. Jamie was dying to see the inside of the house, but knocking at the door was more than even she had the nerve for. Instead, she peeked around the side, where she caught a glimpse of a swimming pool surrounded by a huge flagstone terrace and, of course, more exquisite flower gardens.

Wow, she thought, *their own pool.* Jamie loved to swim, but her family couldn't even afford a membership at the YMCA. What must it be like to be able to roll out of bed and dive into a pool?

Not wanting to press her luck, Jamie headed back to

the car. She had just got herself settled inside when she saw Alison kiss her mother good-bye in the doorway. As Alison walked down the walk, Jamie checked her out. She had to admit that her outfit was pretty cool. No doubt it was one of the many items she had purchased at Poopsie's.

Jamie, hoping no one would notice, was wearing the same dress she had worn to the audition. Her new dress was much too fancy for today, and she wasn't sure if her jeans were right either. Old reliable seemed the most logical, if the most boring, choice.

"Hi, Jamie," Alison said as she climbed into the backseat next to her. "I didn't think I'd see you here."

"Why not? It's a very big limo."

Alison wasn't sure if Jamie was being sarcastic or not. She wore an innocent enough look. "I just didn't know we'd be going together." Embarrassed and terribly self-conscious, Alison turned her head and looked out the window.

Stuck up, Jamie thought, but she was too curious about Alison and her life to let the conversation die. "Nice house," she commented.

"Thank you," Alison said, venturing a shy smile.

"Have you lived there all your life?"

"Since I was two."

Jamie had a mental picture of little Ali picking flowers in her beautiful backyard. How sweet. "What does your father do?"

"He's a lawyer."

"A pretty successful one, I guess."

Alison nodded. "What does your father do?"

Jamie laughed bitterly. "Darned if I know. I haven't seen him in a while."

No wonder she's hostile, Alison thought. There was a lull in the already halting conversation, but Alison couldn't bear the silence, so finally she said, "Do you know what to expect when we get to the studio?"

Jamie shrugged. "They'll take our measurements and maybe show us some sketches for costumes, if they've gotten that far."

"Do you think the other people in the show will be there?" Alison wanted to know. "Will we get to meet them?"

"I haven't a clue."

They were driving through the studio gates. Rows of bungalows lined the street. *These couldn't be the studios,* Alison thought, *they're too small.*

As if in answer to her unasked question, Jamie said, "The producers and writers work in those offices." She was determined to remind Alison that she was the one with all the experience and expertise.

"Where are the studios?"

Jamie pointed ahead. "The soundstages are right over there."

They parked alongside one of the huge buildings. The driver turned and spoke. "Just go in there, make a right, and check in with the secretary. They'll direct you from there."

Alison let Jamie take the lead. They found the secretary, who pointed them in the direction of the costume department. "Ask for Helga," she said.

Helga was waiting for them. "Hello, girls, come right in."

Alison looked around her in amazement. The costume department was a beehive of activity. Sewing machines buzzed in the background, while workers laid out bolts of material on wide tables. Sketches of glamorous costumes covered the walls, many of them bearing the names of famous movies or television shows.

Helga showed them to a large dressing room with a three-way mirror. "Now, girls, I need you to take off your clothes."

Alison and Jamie exchanged glances, actually connecting for a second. This Helga certainly was blunt. "Who should go first?" Alison asked. *Please let it be Jamie,* she prayed.

Helga nodded at Jamie. *Thank you, God,* Alison said silently.

Unconcerned, Jamie pulled her dress over her head. Though they were about the same height, Alison could now see quite clearly that when it came to figures, Jamie was definitely in the Pam department. While Alison tried not to stare, Helga took Jamie's measurements, chattering on about the kind of clothes that Jamie's character, Wendy, might wear.

"She's rich, so I guess she'll have a whole closetful of clothes," Jamie commented.

"I see her in leather skirts and cashmere sweaters."

"Oh, so do I," Jamie agreed fervently.

Then it was Alison's turn to get undressed. She carefully took off her clothes and hung them on the hanger Helga offered. The air conditioning suddenly felt chilly on her body.

Trying to distract herself from the fact that she was standing almost naked in front of a complete stranger—two, if you counted Jamie—Alison asked about her character. "Have you decided about Jane's costumes?"

"Well, from what Ms. Morton and Mr. Greenspan have told me, one of the things Jane doesn't like about Wendy is that Wendy's so rich and she isn't. So, sorry, hon, I guess Jane's clothes aren't going to be so nice."

Some turnaround, Jamie thought as she watched Helga measure Alison. *I get to be the rich one for a change, and Ali has to play the poor relation. I wonder if she's that good an actress?* Then Jamie had a scary thought. Was she a good enough actress to play a rich kid?

Jamie refused to think about that now. She snuck a look at Alison, who did not look at all comfortable standing in her underwear. *She's as slim as a fashion model,* Jamie thought admiringly. *I bet she could wear anything and look great in it.*

Jamie was distracted by a tall, attractive woman coming through the door. She recognized her immediately. This was Donna Wheeler, who was going to play her mother, Amanda Stone, on the show.

"Hello," Donna said with a bright smile. "They told me I'd find you in here, Helga."

"Hello, Ms. Wheeler." Helga greeted her. "I'm just finishing up with your girls."

Donna Wheeler laughed. "We haven't met yet," she said. "Now, who's my daughter, and who's my step-daughter?"

Jamie greeted her shyly. "I'm Jamie. I'll be playing Wendy."

"Well, howdy, daughter," Donna said, giving her a little hug. She went over to Alison. "That makes you Jane. I hope we don't have too many fights. On the show, I mean."

"It's nice to meet you," Alison said politely.

"Have you girls received your first script yet?"

"No," Jamie and Alison said in unison. "Have you?" Jamie asked.

"I just picked it up." She waved a thick binder in the air. "I'm sure if you go over to Kate Morton's office you can pick them up."

Alison finished buttoning her blouse. "I can go get them if you tell me how to get to Kate's office."

Jamie was content to let Alison be the gofer. She wanted to have some time to talk to Donna anyway.

After Alison left, Jamie said, "Do you mind if I ask you a couple of questions, Donna?"

"No, of course not," Donna said. "I'll just let Helga do my fitting while we chat."

Jamie took one of the several chairs in the dressing room. "What sort of a chance do you think this show has of flying?"

"I forgot. You had a long run on *The Happydale Girls.* So naturally, you're wondering how *Sticks and Stones* is going to do."

"It's just that I have a lot of family responsibilities."

Donna immediately looked more sympathetic. "Of course. I have two kids I'm supporting. It's a little easier to plan your life if you know you've got some job security."

"That's it," Jamie answered, relieved that Donna understood.

Turning so Helga could measure her from hip to thigh, Donna said, "Well, you've been around this business long enough to know there are no guarantees. The network has ordered five shows as summer replacements, so we know we'll be paid for those, but—"

"After that, anything can happen," Jamie finished for her.

"I can't kid you, Jamie. Shows go on and off the air all the time. But I think we have a very strong cast, and Kate Morton is one of the best writers in the business."

"I hear she's great. I can't wait to read the script."

"And then there's our director, Rob Stephens." Donna sighed. "He's excellent, too, but a bit of a tyrant, I'm afraid."

"Oh really?" That didn't sound too good.

"Yes, I've worked with him once or twice. He's

good, there's no doubt about that. The thing you have to remember about Rob is that he insists upon doing things his way. He's not too high on actors, especially when they try to put their own interpretations on a part."

"So he gives the directions and we follow," Jamie said.

"That's about right."

Donna went on chattering about other people on the show, but Jamie listened with only half an ear. Donna had said something that had started a small seed growing in her head. Maybe there was a way to get Alison on the wrong side of Rob Stephens and nip her career in the bud.

Jamie had seen enough of Alison Blake to know one thing. Miss Rich Kid didn't deserve this job. For heaven's sake, she had only gotten the part because she had red hair. If she was a brunette, she'd still be sitting in the waiting room. Alison already had it all. There was no reason she should become a TV star, too.

Jamie stared off into space. It just wasn't fair. She had held a job for years, been a success, and then one day, she couldn't get work. Work she really needed. Now, with no experience, Alison had waltzed into an acting role. Jamie could feel righteous indignation flow through her body. Like so many things in life, this was a situation that needed righting. Well, she couldn't do much about most things, but maybe she could do something about this. Of course, she'd have to be careful. The last thing she needed was to cause trouble for herself.

She'd just wait and see. If there was a way to get Alison off the show, she just might go for it.

Chapter 7

Sometimes Alison wondered who was giving this party, anyway. From the moment the kids had talked to her about it, Mrs. Blake had started planning—food, flowers, music. There wasn't a single detail her mother didn't have under control.

She looked across the kitchen table at her mom, who was chewing the eraser end of a pencil, staring down at an already full list of things to do. Mrs. Blake was acting as if she was planning a major battle instead of a party. Well, maybe she was.

"Ali, I've got chicken and ribs." She looked up at her daughter. "Do you think that's enough choices?"

Alison cleared her throat. "Mom, I don't want chicken and ribs."

"What? Why not?"

"Your friends might like chicken and ribs. I think my friends prefer hamburgers and hot dogs. Maybe pizza."

Alison could tell her mother was hurt. Geez, why was it so hard just to tell your parents what you thought? One minute they were telling you to grow up and take responsibility, then, when you expressed a preference for hot dogs over ribs, they took it as a personal slight. "Oh, have whatever you want," Alison said grumpily.

"No, no. I think you're right, Alison," Mrs. Blake responded, running a dark pencil line through the offending foods. "Would you like to work on this together?"

"All right," Alison agreed, though not too quickly.

"I do want your input, sweetheart," her mother assured her. "It's just that you usually like to leave these kinds of details to me."

Alison couldn't very well argue with that. She did leave a lot of things up to her mother. Well, maybe she didn't want to anymore. Her mother wasn't going to be down at the studio to hold her hand, so she'd have to rely more on herself.

That thought had no sooner crossed her mind, when a familiar panicky feeling washed over her. *Concentrate on the party,* Alison advised herself. Picking out colas and food was preferable to thinking about her budding career.

"Well," her mother began, "the caterer is going to have a sweet table out by the pool. It will have all the usual, brownies, cookies, and fixings for ice cream sundaes. Is that okay?"

Alison nodded.

"I'm just not sure about taffy apples." Mrs. Blake chewed the end of her pencil absently.

"Mom, we've had the taffy apple discussion before. I don't think kids will want the caramel all stuck in their teeth." *Especially if they have kissing plans for later,* she thought to herself.

"All right. No taffy apples. Now, what about the napkins. Do you want them to say Alison, or Ali, or just have your initials?"

"I don't really want them to say anything. Can't they just be napkins?"

Her mother frowned. "Just plain pink napkins?"

"Not pink. I'm sick of everyone thinking I'm a pink sort of person. How about black?"

"Black?" Her mother was so startled, Alison finally had to laugh. "All right, maybe that's making too much of a statement. Can we compromise on blue?"

"Blue." Mrs. Blake made a note. "Now we should talk about the deejay."

The discussion went on for another fifteen minutes or so. When Alison felt she had done her duty to her party, she said, "Mom, I've got to study, and I also want to go over the script. I'm nowhere near ready for rehearsal next Monday."

"All right, dear, I understand. But let me just ask you a couple more questions. I know we've sent the invitations out, but is there anyone else you'd like to ask? I need an exact count for the caterer by Friday."

"I've already asked everybody I know, and Dana and Pam have asked the people I don't."

"What about that girl who's going to be on your show?"

"Jamie O'Leary?" Alison asked, startled. "What made you think of her?"

"It would be a nice gesture. She probably won't know anyone but you, of course, but it might be fun for her."

Alison thought about it. Jamie had hardly been what you could call friendly, but they were going to be working together, and she was Alison's age. Besides, it might be fun for Alison's friends to meet a real TV star. Maybe her mother was right.

"I guess I could," she said.

"Good. Why don't you give her a call so I can finalize these numbers."

Alison wasn't sure how to get Jamie's phone number, but she took the phone book out of a drawer and tried to look it up. There were so many O'Learys. Finally, she called Mr. Greenspan's office. The receptionist gave her Jamie's phone number.

Hesitantly, Alison dialed. A little girl answered, "O'Leary residence."

She sounded cute, Alison thought. "Is Jamie there?"

"Yup." She dropped the phone and called out, "Jamie."

When Jamie picked up, Alison said a hurried hello and rushed into the reason for her call.

"You want me to come to your party?" Jamie repeated.

"Yes. I mean, we're going to be seeing a lot of each other . . ."

There was a silence that Alison hurried to fill. "You could bring a date if you want. It'll be fun," she finished limply.

"Can I let you know?"

"Sure. But can you make it soon?" She was about to add that her mother needed to tell the caterer how many kids would be there, but caught herself. She didn't think Jamie would care about her mother's catering problems.

"Yeah. I'll call you back in a couple of hours."

Jamie's thoughts were jumbled as she hung up. This was something. She supposed she ought to feel like Cinderella getting an invitation to the ball. And it was kind of ironic. Here she had spent a lot of her time recently trying to think of a way to get Alison off the show, and Alison was inviting her to a party.

It made Jamie just a little ashamed, but she brushed those feelings aside. So Alison had invited her to a party. So what? It probably made her feel good to offer her a charity invitation. And a date? That was a laugh. Maybe she should just say no.

Then a thought struck her. She was going to be playing a rich girl on the show, and she didn't have a clue about what went on inside a gorgeous house like the Blakes'. Her imagination wasn't that good. She needed do some research, and here Alison was offering it to her on the proverbial silver platter. Could she really pass up this opportunity to get a peek at the life-styles of the rich and wishing-to-be-famous?

Besides, if she was honest, she was intensely curious about Alison, her house, her family, friends, everything. It would be interesting as well as instructive to see what Alison's life was all about.

Jamie debated with herself, but finally curiosity won out. She would go, soak up some of the atmosphere, learn something she could use in her part, and then leave. Maybe she could even figure out just what weaknesses Alison had, so she'd have some ammunition to get her off the show.

Jamie was just about to call Alison back when the phone rang. A male voice that sounded only vaguely familiar said hello and asked for her.

"Who's calling?" she said curtly. She didn't want to be bothered with any salesman.

"Jamie, don't you recognize your dear old dad?"

Jamie stiffened in surprise, but she was determined not to let her father know that she was reacting to his call. "Long time, no hear," she replied with an edge in her voice.

"You lose track of time. You know how it is, kid."

"Actually, I don't. And since you haven't been paying attention, it's been more than a year since you showed up here."

Mr. O'Leary ignored her sarcasm. "How's Elsie and your mother?"

Jamie's laugh was harsh. "They both think you're coming back. I know better."

"Now, hold on, Jamie. Elsie and your mom might have the right idea."

"Another two-day visit? Don't bother."

"I might be persuaded to stay longer."

"Why?" Then, immediately, Jamie knew why. He had heard about her job. "So you found out about *Sticks and Stones*."

"I keep up with the trade papers. But that's not why I'm coming back."

"No? I just bet it isn't. Listen," she said, trying to make her voice sure and definite. "We don't need you here."

"Hey, you can't talk to me like that, Jamie. Where's your mother?"

"Working. Because you're not here to do it." With that, she slammed down the phone.

Elsie came over to her and crawled in her lap. "Jamie, why are you crying?" she asked.

"I'm not," Jamie lied, wiping a tear from her eye.

"You look sad."

"Mad."

"Who are you mad at?"

Jamie didn't know if she should tell her. Did she really want to tell a four-year-old kid her father was a total jerk? "No one you know," Jamie finally said. And in an odd sort of way, that was the truth.

As she set the table for dinner, Jamie tried to decide if she should tell her mother about the phone call. She'd want to know, that was for sure. But if she told her about the call, Mrs. O'Leary would probably get her hopes up, driving Jamie crazy with her plans about what was going to happen when Jack came back.

As it turned out, the decision was taken out of her hands. When Mrs. O'Leary came home after work that night, the first thing she asked was if they had gotten any calls.

Before Jamie could say anything, Elsie said, "Someone called and made Jamie cry."

"What's this?" Mrs. O'Leary asked, turning toward Jamie with a concerned look.

"I wasn't crying. I told Elsie that."

"You had tears in your eyes. I saw you. Your eyes was wet," Elsie insisted stoutly.

"Your daughter is exaggerating," Jamie said.

"But did someone call?"

"That girl Alison from the show. She asked me to a party on Saturday night."

"How nice!"

Jamie stuck a grape into her mouth. "I guess."

"But that couldn't have been the call that made you cry."

"How many times do I have to tell you? I wasn't crying. Are you going to believe a four-year-old over me?"

Glancing over at the table, Jamie could see her sister pouting. "I'm not lying," Elsie said.

It wasn't really fair to have Elsie take the rap, Jamie thought. "Maybe I did feel a little bad after one of the calls."

"Why?" her mother queried.

Jamie glanced in Elsie's direction. "I'll tell you later."

It was eight o'clock before Elsie was tucked into bed. The moment Mrs. O'Leary walked out of the bedroom she asked, "So, tell me about the call that upset you this afternoon. Who was it?"

Gritting her teeth, Jamie said, "My so-called father."

"Jack?"

"You mean there might be a chance someone else is my father?"

"Jamie, that's not funny." Mrs. O'Leary looked so hurt Jamie instantly regretted her sarcasm.

"Mom, I figured out why he called. He didn't even try to deny it." It was important to Jamie that her mother listen to her for once.

"He wants to see us, right?"

Jamie hated the excited expression on her mother's face. "Oh, he wants to see us, now that I'm going to be working on television again."

"Your father said that?" Mrs. O'Leary looked doubtful.

"Not exactly . . ."

"Well, there." Relief passed over her mother's face. "He just misses us."

"Mom, who's the kid here, you or me? He misses the money."

"I won't hear that," her mother said, getting up and heading for the kitchen.

Jamie followed her. "Why not? It's the truth."

"Oh, Jamie, of course it isn't. Someday when you're older maybe you'll understand. Your father is a good man. He was the best for you—you don't remember how good he was. Not just when you were a *Happydale* girl, either. He is your father, he loves you, and . . . and I know you love him, too, Jamie. Did he say when he was coming?"

"I hung up on him before he could tell me."

"Hung up! Oh, Jamie, how could you?"

"Don't worry," Jamie said, sarcasm dripping from her voice. "He'll call back."

Mrs. O'Leary didn't seem to get it. "When?" she asked.

Jamie threw up her hands. "Hopefully not for a long, long time." She grabbed her coat and headed downstairs. The apartment suddenly seemed smaller than usual.

It was still light out, plenty light enough to see the garbage strewn in the streets. They were going to have to do something about moving. If the show took off, she couldn't have the tabloids find out she lived in such an awful place. She supposed she'd have to take care of finding an apartment and getting them moved, too. Usually that was the kind of thing that parents did, but it was clear to Jamie that the only adult in this family was her. She bit back a sob. *Why me?* she thought savagely.

Mrs. Blake appeared in Alison's doorway. "The guests are starting to arrive."

"Not yet!" Alison yelped. "I'm not ready."

"Sure you are. And you look beautiful."

Alison stared at her full-length mirror. She could barely believe this hot-looking girl in the mirror was her. In her new, tight, slinky dress, and her mother's good pearls, Alison felt completely reborn.

"Who's here?" Alison asked, pulling herself away from the mirror.

"Dana and a few kids I don't know."

"Is everything ready?"

"All set up."

Maybe this was going to be fun after all.

Mr. Blake poked his head in the door. "Is this my little girl?" he asked.

Tonight the comment didn't annoy her. "I guess so," Alison giggled.

Mr. Blake shook his head. "Can't believe it. That Dan Greenspan's obviously a lot smarter than he looks. The doorbell keeps ringing, kiddo. You'd better get downstairs."

The party was getting off the ground, most of the action happening around the pool. The deejay was already taking requests for songs. Dana, Pam, Elliot, and several other kids greeted Alison.

"You look fabulous," Dana said.

"You, too."

Elliot gave her a wolf whistle. "Wait until Brad gets a look at you."

"Where is Brad?" Alison asked.

"He's coming with Steve. Steve has a little surprise

of his own."

The kids continued to pour in, but Alison was very aware that neither Brad and Steve, nor Jamie, had showed up. Could it be that Jamie had decided not to come at all?

Even without Brad, Alison found herself having a surprisingly good time. Ever since word had spread around the school about her role as Jane, kids she didn't even know had been coming up to her, offering their congratulations. Just when she was leaving Madison High, it felt for the first time she was really at the center of things.

Alison was headed toward the kitchen when she heard the front doorbell ring. "I'll get it," she called to the housekeeper. Opening the door, Alison gave a small gasp of surprise. There stood Jamie, wearing the exact same dress that she had on.

"Oh, my goodness!" Jamie looked shocked, too.

"I can't believe it. Did you get this dress at Poopsie's?"

"Yes." *My one big purchase,* Jamie thought grimly.

Alison looked jealously at how fabulously Jamie filled out her dress. She looked so sophisticated—and sexy. The guys would go nuts over her.

She's totally elegant, Jamie thought as she gave Alison the once-over. *She looks so different from the shy little girl I saw at the costume fitting.*

"Well, come on in," Alison said. "I guess the kids will get a laugh out of it."

Swell, being laughed at by a bunch of snobs. I

can't wait. Jamie followed her inside.

"Well, they won't mistake us for twins. Your French braid is cool," Alison told her. *Am I babbling?* Alison thought nervously as Jamie followed her through the house.

Jamie took in Alison's house as they walked out to the patio. The huge entry hall with its winding staircase was probably bigger than Jamie's whole apartment.

"Well, let me introduce you around."

Jamie hadn't been expecting much from Alison's friends, but she had forgotten that telling people you were an actress was a great conversation opener. The kids did laugh at the sight of her and Ali wearing the same dress, but it was all nice and friendly. Most of them remembered *The Happydale Girls* or had at least seen it in reruns, so much of what they asked revolved around that show.

"Whatever happened to that girl who played the oldest orphan?" Pam inquired.

Jamie lowered her voice to a confidential whisper. "Drugs."

"Is she in jail?" one of the boys wanted to know.

Jamie shook her head. "No, but she can't really work anymore."

"Wow," Dana said. "This is great, getting all the inside dish." After a few more minutes of gossiping, though, she pulled Jamie away from her admiring circle. "Can I talk to you a second?"

"Sure."

"I don't know if you're aware of this, but I was the one who came to audition for the show that day. Ali was just along for moral support."

"Yes. I heard."

"Well, I don't hold anything against Alison, but I still want to get my own career happening."

Jamie knew where this was going. Like lots of opportunists, Dana was going to ask her about a job.

"I've already told Alison to keep her ears open for, like, guest parts or something."

"Well, then I will, too." *Not!* Jamie added to herself.

"Great! Boy, you two are so lucky. Alison's sort of going nuts about this thing, but I guess you'll be a big help to her."

Jamie didn't say anything.

"I don't know how Alison would handle it if she had to work with people who weren't nice," Dana continued.

Now, this was getting interesting. "Well, like I told you at Poopsie's, there are plenty of creeps in show business."

Dana shrugged. "Ali's awfully sensitive."

"Doesn't stand up for herself?" Jamie suggested.

"Not really."

Is that so? Jamie thought.

"I'm not sure Ali could handle it if things get rough," Dana confided.

Jamie smiled. "Don't worry about her, Dana. I'll take care of Alison."

Dana looked relieved. "Oh, good. She'd feel terrible if she blew this."

Jamie caught sight of two boys coming through the door. The shorter one was cute enough. But the taller one, with the surfer haircut, was an absolute doll. "Who's that?" Jamie asked, trying to sound casual.

Dana followed Jamie's glance. "Steve Kaye and Brad D'amato. Brad's the to-die-for one." She made a face. "Steve's the one that likes me."

"Not interested, huh?"

"Not my type." Dana shrugged.

"What about Brad?"

"Oh, he's everyone's type, right? But he's taken. He's Ali's boyfriend."

Of course. What is this girl, a princess out of a fairy tale? Jamie asked herself. *Along with everything money can buy, she's got the cutest guy in the room.*

"They've been going together about six months," Dana continued.

"They . . . they don't seem like the same type."

Dana laughed. "I guess not. Brad's a pretty dynamic guy. He's always on, if you know what I mean. I suppose you could even say he's wild."

Jamie arched an eyebrow.

"Oh, I don't mean he does drugs or anything, but he's ready to have fun, go crazy whenever anybody says the word."

What does he see in little Alison? Jamie was dying to ask, but she couldn't quite figure out a way to make the question come out right. She didn't have to worry. Dana was already into the story of how the two of them got together. "We have this study buddy program at the high school . . ."

"Study buddies?" Jamie tried to hide a smile.

"It's a geeky name, I know, but it works pretty well. If you're not doing well in a subject, you can sign up to get a tutor. Usually it's someone older, but in their case, Ali is this brain in English, and Brad doesn't know a verb from a semicolon."

"So she tutored him, got him an A, and the rest is history?"

"Something like that. Only it was a C. Still, even that was a minor miracle for Brad. He always dated girls like him, you know, fast. I think Alison is kind of a novelty for him."

"How does he feel about her being on television?"

"Well, he tries to act like he's cool about it, but I don't think he likes it." Dana waved to someone. "Listen, there's someone I haven't said hello to yet. He's on the football team. Want to meet him?"

"No, thanks. I think I'll wander around for a while."

"Okay. Later. And thanks for keeping me in mind for any parts that come up, Jamie."

Jamie smiled. Then she turned and headed in Brad's direction. As she had so many other times lately, Jamie noticed male eyes widening as they caught sight of her. She pulled her shoulders back and casually flipped her braid over one shoulder.

"Hello," she said. "I'm Jamie O'Leary."

"The one on Alison's show," Brad said, smiling.

"Or she's the one on mine," Jamie countered. Their locked look was interrupted by Brad's friend.

"I'm Steve." He stuck out his hand.

Jamie looked at it with amusement and then shook. She turned to Brad. "And you're? . . ." she asked, pretending not to know.

"Brad."

"Oh, Alison's boyfriend!"

Brad shrugged.

Turning to Steve, Jamie said, "I've heard rumors you have a surprise for everyone."

"How did you know?" Steve asked.

"I get around," Jamie replied with a wink.

"Well, I was going to have everyone come outside and have a look, but I suppose I could give you a preview."

"We could," Brad cut in.

"Hey, it's not *your* car," Steve protested.

"A new car," Jamie said. "That's terrific."

"Wait till you see it." Steve's voice was full of enthusiasm. "It really is terrific."

Jamie turned to Brad. "Let's go."

They headed out to the driveway, packed with automobiles. There were plenty of cool-looking Jeeps and sporty compacts, but a bright red, low-slung convertible sports car at the end of the driveway stood out.

"That's yours?"

Steve looked a little embarrassed. "Yeah. I swore I

wasn't going to go for anything so flashy, but I guess I couldn't help myself."

"I can see why," Jamie murmured.

They went over to take a closer look. Jamie ran her hand over the smooth exterior and then lightly touched the top of the leather seat. In her TV days, she had seen plenty of nice cars, but it had been a while since she had been this close to one. She had come over to the two boys to get to know Brad, but she wouldn't mind having a ride in this beautiful machine.

After they had *ooh*ed and *aah*ed over the car for a while, they went back in the house. The romantic music out by the pool sounded very enticing. "Have you danced with Alison yet?" Jamie asked Brad politely.

"No. But I haven't danced with you yet, either."

Jamie could see out of the corner of her eye the surprised look Steve gave Brad.

"I don't know . . ."

Brad tugged at her hand. "Come on."

They left Steve in the hallway as they headed out to the patio. Alison was dancing, as were most of the other kids. Brad pulled Jamie out to the dance area and began moving in time to the slow music that was playing.

"Brad, I don't want to get Alison upset," Jamie said, half-hoping she was doing just that. "I barely know her."

"Hey, all we're doing is dancing. Besides, Alison and I are free agents."

"That's not the way I heard it."

"She's going off to be a big actress. She certainly

can't get mad just because I danced with her co-star."

"I guess not," Jamie answered, snuggling closer.

They danced quietly for a while, then Brad said, "Don't get me wrong. I like Ali a lot."

"You're just mad that she's decided to take this part."

Brad looked at her in amazement. "How did you know? I haven't even said that to Ali yet."

"I could just tell you're upset," Jamie said sympathetically.

"It's not her thing," he said more forcefully. "I don't know why she's even doing this."

"Who wouldn't want to be on a televison show?"

"She's not the type," Brad said stubbornly.

"I know. She's shy. And sensitive."

Brad pulled back and looked at her. "What are you, psychic?"

"Maybe."

"Psychic and very cute."

This guy moves fast, Jamie thought. Getting the subject back on track, she said, "You're going to have to get used to Alison on the show, Brad. Rehearsals start Monday."

"Well, I just think it's a bad idea. Alison will freak once this show starts."

Jamie smiled up at him. "Don't worry. I'm going to keep my eye on her."

"You are?"

"Oh, yes. Like I told Dana, I'm going to take care of Alison."

Chapter 8

Dana was staying over at Alison's. Even though they were both exhausted from the long, exciting evening of partying, they couldn't stop talking long enough to go to sleep.

Feeling cozy in her flowered cotton pajamas, Alison sprawled on her bed while Dana, in a wild Day-Glo nightshirt, did exercises on the floor.

"Can't you do that in the morning?"

"I always exercise before I go to bed," Dana huffed.

"You got enough exercise dancing."

"I haven't done my leg lifts yet. Besides, I ate two sundaes. Two!"

Alison shrugged. "So tomorrow, you'll eat less."

"Easy for you to say. You're like a model. You never gain an ounce."

"I'm a little too thin, don't you think?" She looked down at herself. "Especially, well, you know where."

"I'm sure the costuming department can fix that up," Dana said, finally falling down, exhausted.

"Jamie doesn't need any help in that department," Alison said. "Did you see her in *our* dress? She sure filled it out better than I did."

"So what? You're the one with the figure like the girls in the magazines."

"Brad seemed to like the way she looked in it," Alison replied quietly.

"Oh, so they danced once or twice."

"Three times. He danced with me twice."

"You don't have to worry about Jamie O'Leary," Dana said. "He'll never see her again."

"No, but I will," Alison said glumly.

Dana examined her nails. "I thought she was kind of nice."

"You did? What makes you say that?"

"She offered to help me get a part on your show."

Alison looked at Dana doubtfully. This didn't sound like the Jamie she was getting to know. The only thing Jamie had really said to her other than hello and good-bye was to ask whether she and Brad were a steady item or whether they saw other people. Alison hadn't thought she was asking out of simple curiosity and had hemmed and hawed a noncommittal answer. Now, it seemed as if Jamie was trying to win Dana over as well—and she was succeeding.

"I don't know if Jamie can really get anyone a part," Alison said carefully.

"Oh, not yet, maybe. But remember, she's been

around this business for a while. She might have lots of contacts."

"Then why was she in Mr. Greenspan's office, just like you?"

Dana got up and crawled into the bed next to Alison's. "Why are you so hard on her, Ali? She was just trying to have fun at the party. If I were you, I'd be nice to Jamie. You're going on this show as a total novice. You're going to need all the help you can get."

Dana's words kept swirling around Alison's head as she tried to fall asleep. Who was she kidding? She had practically forced her parents to let her take the job, then she had gotten caught up in the excitement of costume fittings and studying the first script, but now that shooting was about to start, it was time to face facts. Alison felt in her heart of hearts that she was going to flop, and flop bigtime. She didn't have a lick of experience, and except for Mr. Greenspan's enthusiasm, there was no proof that she had an ounce of talent, either.

Maybe Dana was right, Alison thought as she punched her pillow, trying to find a more comfortable spot. If she wasn't going to humiliate herself, she'd have to do something. Jamie could be an enormous help. Sure, she had seemed a little snippy sometimes, but she had never really done anything mean. Jamie couldn't help it if Brad was attracted to her, and she was probably just trying to be polite when Dana asked her for a job.

There was only one thing to do. She was going to

have to make Jamie her friend, watch how she acted on the set, and follow any advice she would give. Alison stared up at the ceiling. Otherwise, she was dead meat.

Alison learned one thing during the next week. No matter how much you dreaded a day, it eventually arrived. Here she was sitting next to her father, driving toward the studio. It didn't seem quite real.

She took a small mirror out of her pocketbook and glanced at it. She hadn't had a good night's sleep in so long, she probably looked like a zombie by now. To her surprise, you couldn't tell by looking. Her skin had a nice flush to it that was probably just nerves, but gave her a healthy glow all the same.

"You look beautiful," Mr. Blake said, watching her.

"Oh, Dad." Quickly, she shoved the mirror back in her purse.

"You'll see. Everyone will think that."

"Yeah, they'll think I'm some airhead who doesn't know how to speak a line," Alison said, finally confessing all her fears.

Mr. Blake shook his head. "Sweetie, you wouldn't be normal if you weren't having a few doubts."

"A few!" Alison wasn't sure whether the strangled noise in her throat was a laugh or a sob.

"Now listen, Alison. You know what I think about this idea. I'm still not sure why I'm letting you do this. It goes against everything I believe about raising a child. But you and your mother know how to wrap me around your little fingers."

"With some help from Dan Greenspan."

"Yeah, he made a difference, too. We can still turn this car around and go home. If it gets impossible, I can get you out of your contract. But I won't have you walking in there believing you're not any good. First of all, Dan wouldn't have chosen you if he thought you'd flop. You've already had a couple of coaching sessions with him. He's always praised you, right?"

Alison nodded.

"So there you are. Second, if you have confidence in yourself, other people will, too. Part of this is attitude."

"Attitude?"

"Sure. Do you think I walk into court thinking I'm going to lose a case? Do I tell my client, 'Gee, I'll do the best I can, but it probably won't do any good'?"

Alison had to smile. Her father was probably the most self-assured man she knew. "Guess not."

"Of course not," he said emphatically. "I act like I'm the best darn lawyer in Los Angeles, and everyone else starts to think I am, too."

"But Dad, you've got the education, the experience . . ."

"You'll have the experience, too, one day. Then you won't need the confidence as much as you do right now."

Alison leaned over and gave her father a kiss on the cheek.

"Hey, what was that for?"

"You don't even want me to do this show, and you're still telling me how to make a go of it."

"You know what Davy Crockett said."

"Actually, I don't."

"Be sure you're right. Then go ahead."

Alison still wasn't sure her decision was right, but she went ahead and marched right up to the sound-stage where *Sticks and Stones* was going to be taped, pulled herself up to her full height, and went in. Sets were still being built, and the sound of hammers and saws made a steady background buzz. A long, square table surrounded by chairs sat in one corner. In another was a smaller table covered with doughnuts, juice, coffee, etcetera. Donna Wheeler was standing there, putting a jelly doughnut on a plate.

"Hi," Alison said coming up to her, glad to see a friendly face.

"Well, hello. Ready to get started?"

"As ready as I'll ever be."

"Try not to sound as if you're on your way to the guillotine."

"This is my first show," Alison confided.

"I heard. But don't worry. Everyone had a first show once."

Mr. Greenspan walked over to them. "Oh good, another arrival. Have you studied your script, Alison?"

"I memorized the whole thing," Alison told him proudly.

Mr. Greenspan looked surprised. "You didn't have to be word perfect today. Did I forget to tell you that? I'm sorry." He looked so concerned.

"No no, you did tell me. I just thought it would be a good idea," Alison hastened to explain.

"That's okay. But we do make changes. Are you a quick study?"

"I don't know," she said helplessly.

"Now don't make the girl nervous, Dan," Donna Wheeler said. "I'm sure she'll be able to handle anything we throw at her."

Alison was glad Donna was so sure.

"Of course, she will." Mr. Greenspan patted Alison's arm. "That's why I hired her. Alison, why don't we go over and meet the rest of the cast?"

Alison dutifully followed Mr. Greenspan over to the large table, where a gray-haired man in his forties and a guy who looked to be about eighteen sat talking. With his wavy brown hair and dark brooding eyes, the eighteen-year-old was a real hunk.

"Alison, I'd like you to meet your dad, Joe Stickley. In real life he's Benjamin Epson," Dan said, indicating the older man.

"Oh, I know you," Alison said. "You were on *Crisis Hospital.* I loved that show—so did all my friends."

"Yes, like that commercial says, I'm not a doctor in real life, but I play one on television," Ben laughed. "I'm not a father either, but I guess I'll be playing yours."

"And this is your brother, Lucas, otherwise known as Mike Malone," Mr. Greenspan said.

Mike stuck out his hand, and Alison shook it tentatively.

"I'm sure you haven't seen me in anything. Unless you're good at remembering extras in movies."

"You haven't seen me in anything, either, unless you've been hanging around Madison High." She might as well let everyone know she was a total newcomer. Maybe that way they wouldn't expect too much from her.

Mike laughed. It was a nice laugh, warm and friendly.

"Let's see," Mr. Greenspan continued, "you've already met Donna, and of course Jamie."

"Yes."

"Then there's only one more cast member to meet." He looked around. "Is Rodney here yet?"

Ben and Mike shook their heads.

"Well, let me introduce you to some other people, and we'll see if we can find Rodney."

By the time Mr. Greenspan was done, Alison's head was whirling. She had met Rob Stephens, the director, some of the writers, the script girl, the lighting designer, and several of the technical people.

"Wow, I had no idea so many people worked on a television show," she said, still a little shell-shocked from all the new faces.

Mr. Greenspan laughed. "That's not the half of them. There's the floor director, the comedian who warms up the audience, a set designer, the continuity girl, the stagehands . . ."

Alison just shook her head.

"And here comes Rodney."

Alison thought the boy coming toward her looked a little like a smaller version of Steve. He was small and thin and wore big tortoiseshell glasses. His dark hair was plastered down, but a few cowlicks had escaped. The woman walking beside him was nodding intently as Rodney talked.

"He was perfect for the role," Mr. Greenspan whispered. "A real little know-it-all. And he's like a miniature grown-up. We're even calling the kid in the show Rodney because the name just seems to fit so well."

"Hello," Rodney said as he came up to them. "I don't believe this young lady and I have met."

Mr. Greenspan gave Alison a look as if to say, *See what I mean?*

Alison offered her hand. "No. I'm Alison Blake."

"And will you be playing my sister or my stepsister?" he asked seriously as he shook her hand.

"I'm Jane Stickley. One of the middle-class ones."

"Oh, I play Rodney Stone. But I'm sure we'll have many scenes together."

"I'm sure."

"And this is Rodney's mother, Mrs. Janeway," Dan Greenspan said. "You know, she'll be serving as your chaperon, too."

"Oh, I heard something about that." Alison had been told that any minors under age sixteen needed a chaperon on the set. Mrs. Janeway had agreed to serve as the chaperon for Alison, Jamie, and Rodney, so the girls wouldn't have to find anyone to come to the set with them. "How do you do, Mrs. Janeway?"

Mrs. Janeway nodded at Alison and remarked, "Hello, dear. I know chaperoning you won't be a problem. But I assure you, I will be here if you need me." It was clear where Rodney got his manner.

"Thank you," Alison said, trying to stifle a smile. Briefly, she wondered how Mrs. Janeway and Jamie would get along. Come to think of it, where was Jamie? She hadn't seen her yet.

Jamie stood at a sink in the ladies' room, splashing cold water on her face. *It's a good thing Alison can't see me now,* she thought. *What a laugh. I'm supposed to be the pro, and I'm in the bathroom getting sick.*

She would have liked to convince herself that she had caught a flu bug or eaten something that didn't agree with her, but Jamie knew that she was throwing up from nerves, pure and simple. She had been queasy since she woke up this morning, and when she arrived at the studio, she had headed right to the restroom.

At least no one else had come in. That would have been a major embarrassment. She felt better now, thank heavens.

Taking a deep breath, she walked back out into the studio. Kate Morton, the head writer greeted her. "Where have you been, Jamie? I've been worried about you." She peered at Jamie. "You look flushed. Are you okay?"

"I'm fine," Jamie assured her. "Ready to rock and roll."

"Well, let's get started. You still have a few people to meet. Then we're going to start our reading run-through."

Almost everyone was sitting at the table by the time Kate made the introductions. Jamie tried to look nonchalant as she took her assigned seat next to Alison, who seemed perfectly at ease. She felt better when Alison unexpectedly turned to her and whispered, "I'm scared to death."

Jamie resisted the urge to say, *Me too.* Instead, she replied, "You'll be fine." If she was going to get Alison off this show, she was going to have to win her confidence first.

"Thanks," Alison said gratefully.

Mr. Greenspan rapped his water glass for attention. "For those of you who don't know how this works, we're going to start at the beginning of the script and read it all the way through. You don't have to throw yourself into acting right now, but Kate, Rob, and I want to get ideas about how you interact and how the script is working. As you know, the first scene takes place at the Stickleys' house, the next one at the Stones', and the third one at the garage. Then we have each of the parents preparing for their first date. The first exchange is between Alison and Mike. So Mike, you've got the first line. Why don't you begin?"

Alison wished she didn't have to be in the opening scene, but there was no getting out of this now. Mike said his line and she responded. To her surprise, in a few moments she was lost in the part. She was no longer

Alison Blake, but Jane Stickley, trading wisecracks with her brother, Lucas. This must be why people loved acting. You really could become someone else.

Before she knew it, they had gone all the way through the script. Alison had no idea if she had been any good, but she had enjoyed herself. She could hardly wait to start again.

"Let's break for lunch," Mr. Greenspan said. "But, Alison, Jamie, and Rodney, I want to see you three for a moment."

Well, Alison reasoned, *if she had done something wrong, so had the others.* At least, she wasn't being singled out.

"I hope you three haven't forgotten about school," Mr. Greenspan said when they had gathered around him.

"I love school," Rodney piped up.

"Yes, I'm sure of that," Mr. Greenspan laughed. "After lunch, we'll come back here for a while, then you three have to spend some time being tutored by your teacher, Mrs. Haley."

"You mean we'll all have the same teacher?" Alison asked with surprise.

"Yes, she's certified to teach all the grades." Mr. Greenspan smiled. "Don't worry, Alison. Mrs. Haley knows you're past fractions. She's got some geometry for you."

"I'm past fractions, too," Rodney informed him.

"I'm not surprised. Now head over to the commissary and get some lunch," Mr. Greenspan told them.

Alison decided it was a good thing that Rodney was with them, chattering every step of the way. She and Jamie didn't seem have much to say to each other, even though there were things they could have talked about, like the party. Alison wasn't even sure that Jamie would sit with her.

After they had gone through the line, Jamie turned to her and said, "I'm going to sit with Mike. He's over there, alone."

Before Alison could say anything, Rodney said, "Yes, good idea. We can all discuss how the morning's reading went."

Jamie made a face. Alison hadn't been part of her plans, much less Rodney. But it was also clear there was no way to get away from him, so Jamie went over to Mike's table with Alison and Rodney trailing behind her.

"Have a seat," Mike said.

"Thank you," Rodney answered for all of them. "So, how do you think it went this morning?"

"Oh, I don't have much experience in these things," Mike said seriously. "How do you think it went?"

"Superlatively," Rodney answered. "I can see we're really beginning to jell as a group."

"Glad you think so," Jamie said, taking a sip of her soup, the only thing she felt she could eat.

"You sound like you've been around television before, Rodney," Alison said.

"Movies."

"Movies?" Jamie repeated.

"Yes. I starred in *Baby Makes Three*."

"Hey, I saw that," Alison said. "But who were you?"

"The baby, of course."

"But the baby was a girl," Alison remembered.

For the first time all day, Rodney didn't seem quite so adult. He looked like the embarrassed little kid that he was. "I know. But the producers thought I was the cutest baby that auditioned."

"How does a baby audition?" Mike asked with a grin. "Spit up and make in his pants?"

"I was also in *Aliens from the Planet Zero*," Rodney put in hastily, "but I wore a lot of makeup in that, so you might not recognize me," Rodney continued. "And two years ago I was in that movie, *Jetsetters*. I was one of the children."

Jamie looked at him intently. "I did see you in that. You were the obnoxious one, right?"

Rodney nodded.

"Well, you'd better be careful not to get typecast, kid," she added.

Alison thought Jamie was being a little mean, but all Rodney did was nod wisely and say, "That's so true."

Mike took a sip of his drink. "The boy must have something. He's got better credits than I do."

"Better than me, too," Alison added.

Jamie sipped her soup. Rodney's movie career notwithstanding, she was the one with all the acting experience in this group. It made her feel a little better. Not much, but a little.

For a while they discussed the script as they ate. "I'm supposed to be such a goody-goody," Alison remarked.

Typecasting again, Jamie thought, but all she said was. "Yeah, I could see where that could get a little boring for you."

"And I'm this big athlete." Mike shook his head. "I hope they never actually want me to do anything on the field."

"You aren't good at sports?" Jamie asked with surprise.

"Throw any sort of ball at me and watch me drop it. I do lift weights, but that's about it."

Jamie turned to Alison. "Your boyfriend is a big athlete, I hear." She wanted to make it clear to Mike that Alison was already spoken for. Mike was too cute to give Alison a chance at him.

Alison nodded. "Football."

"Do you two know each other?" Mike asked, looking from Jamie to Alison.

"We met right after the audition. Alison asked me to a party at her house," Jamie said lightly. "I met her boyfriend, Brad, there."

"What about you?" Mike asked. "Do you have a boyfriend?"

"Nope," Jamie responded, smiling. She was about to ask Mike the same question when Rodney piped up. "I have a girlfriend."

Who cares? Jamie thought, but Alison said, "Really. Is she nice?"

"Extremely nice and quite pretty. Unfortunately, she's not too good in school."

"A little lacking in the brain department?" Mike inquired.

"Just a little."

"Well, it would be hard to compete with you," Mike replied.

Mike was being slightly sarcastic, Alison knew, but later, as Jamie, Rodney, and Alison sat in the area designated as their school, she wondered what Mike would think if he could see Rodney now. Although he was only nine, he was fluent in Spanish, and he seemed to know more math than she and Jamie put together. Their teacher, Mrs. Haley, a short, stocky woman with tightly curled hair, seemed positively delirious that such a remarkable student had turned up in her class.

"Well, Rodney, it certainly isn't usual, but I believe we're going to have you doing some of the same work as the high schoolers," she said with a smile.

"Thank you," Rodney said gravely.

Oh great, Jamie thought, trying not to scowl. Not only would she have to put up with Alison, who from all she'd heard was sure to be a better student than her, but now there was little Albert Einstein to compete with.

"How long will we have to be in school?" Alison asked.

"The law requires four hours a day, but Mr. Greenspan told me he wants you in here whenever you're not needed on the set."

"That should take up a lot of time," Rodney noted.

Everything took up a lot of time, Alison thought, as she walked in the door of her house that evening. She had already gotten three pages of script changes, an hour of homework, and Mr. Greenspan had asked her to spend some time walking around the room with a book on her head, so she would remember to stand up straight.

"How was it?" her mother asked, coming out of the living room. "I was hoping you'd have a chance during the day to call."

Alison shook her head wearily. "Not a second."

Mrs. Blake led her over to the couch. "Your dad has to work late, but he wanted me to get all the details. Are you hungry?"

"I'm too tired to be hungry. Besides, I've got homework, and line changes to learn."

"I'll make up a tray. You can eat in your bedroom, if you like."

Alison gave her mother a quick hug. "I think I'll take you up on that," she said.

"And while you're eating, you can tell me everything, okay?"

Nodding, Alison headed upstairs. She had been talking all day. She hoped she'd have enough energy to move her mouth by the time her mother came upstairs with the tray.

Alison had barely pulled off her dress when the phone rang. She thought it might be Brad, or maybe Dana, checking in with her. But to her surprise,

Jamie's voice came over the line. "Jamie, hi. What's up?"

"I was wondering. Since we only have to work for half a day tomorrow, maybe we could get together and run some of our lines."

Alison's heart rose. Jamie had been wonderful at rehearsal. Even though the group had just been sitting around the table, without makeup or costumes, Jamie really had become Wendy Stone. She sounded different, even looked different. Alison had enjoyed reading the lines, but she knew that she hadn't transformed herself the way Jamie had.

"Alison?" Jamie's voice broke into the silence.

"Oh, I'm sorry, Jamie. I was just thinking about how good you were today. I would love it if you wanted to go over the script with me."

"Run some lines," Jamie corrected. "That's the correct term."

"Run some lines," Alison repeated.

"So we'll just leave together after rehearsal tomorrow?"

"Sure. Do you want to come here, or should we go to your house?"

Oh yeah, Jamie thought. *Let's go over to my house. I'll just make sure I put my bed back in the couch, and we can settle in and get to work.* Out loud, she said, "No, your house would be better."

"All right," Alison said agreeably.

"I have some ideas on the way you should do your part," Jamie said.

"Really? I could use some help."

"I'll tell you about them tomorrow."

"Great!" Alison said enthusiastically. "See you tomorrow."

"Okay. Bye."

Jamie hung up the phone and stared into space. *Step one accomplished,* Jamie told herself. *Alison trusts me. This may be easier than I thought. If Alison takes all the good advice I'm about to offer, she'll be off the show before she knows what hit her!*

Chapter 9

"I'm glad you told me to bring my bathing suit," Jamie said to Alison, as she made herself more comfortable on the lounge chair. Looking around, Jamie wished yet again that she could live like this. If she were rich, she'd have a house as big as this, but instead of just a swimming pool, there would be a tennis court, too. And instead of the house being here in the suburbs, she'd have it down at Malibu overlooking the Pacific Ocean. That way she could walk on the beach every day.

"Are you a good swimmer?" Alison asked.

"Not really, I just paddle around. No one ever taught me."

"Oh. My dad taught me when I was just a toddler."

I'll bet he did. Jamie averted her head. All her father had ever taught her was how to get up early so she could be at the studio on time.

Alison passed Jamie the sunscreen. "We'd better use

a lot of this. I'm sure Mr. Greenspan would go nuts if we both got sunburned."

"Yeah. Two redheads. We'd look like lobsters."

Alison smiled. Jamie had been so nice today. Friendly and really helpful. Not hostile at all, the way she could be sometimes. "So how do you think I did, going over . . . I mean running my lines," she corrected herself.

"Pretty good," Jamie replied.

Alison detected a certain lack of enthusiasm. "I've got a long way to go, huh?"

"I wouldn't say that." Jamie knew she was going to have to play the rest of her game very carefully. She didn't want to arouse Alison's suspicions. "You read well."

"Sounds like a *but* is about to follow."

Jamie acted like she didn't want to say more.

"Tell me," Alison said. "What's the *but*?"

"*But,* have you thought much about the character of Jane?"

"Sure I have."

"Then who is she?"

Alison looked at Jamie, perplexed. "She's supposed to be a nice, sweet kid, isn't she?"

"That's how you've been playing her, all right."

"That's how Mr. Greenspan described her."

Jamie shrugged.

"But you think that's wrong." Alison made it more of a statement than a question.

"Well, I don't think it's very interesting."

"I don't know how else to do it," Alison said helplessly. "You and Rodney have all the best lines."

Jamie took a sip of her soda. "Yeah, I agree. They are making you and Mike a little bland. Of course, he's so gorgeous . . . he'll have girls tuning in just to look."

"I'll probably fade into the wallpaper." Alison could feel her confidence oozing away.

"You don't have to let that happen," Jamie counseled.

"I can't go to Kate Morton and ask her to write me new lines. She'd think I was terrible."

"It's not a matter of new lines. You can read the ones you have differently."

Alison looked bewildered.

"It's called making a part your own."

Alison handed her script to Jamie. "Show me what you mean."

Jamie flipped through a few pages. "Here. You're supposed to tell Mike you think it's great that your dad has a date with my mother. Now, you've been reading the line straight. But what if you added a sarcastic edge to the whole thing? Like, *right, it would be great.* Then the audience won't think you're such a dope."

"A dope?"

"Sure. What kid wants her parent dating like a teenager?"

"That's true," Alison said slowly.

"You can add some dimension to Jane, make people see that you've got something on the ball."

Alison took back the script and started looking through it. "I guess there's lots of places where I could do that sort of thing."

Jamie tried not to look too eager. "Sure, I could go over it with you, if you like."

"But what if Mr. Greenspan, or Mr. Stephens, doesn't want me to read the part that way?" Alison said, looking up. "Kate Morton might be really insulted if I tried to change the role from the way she wrote it."

Jamie had hoped that tiny detail wouldn't occur to Alison, but she had prepared for it just in case. "I've been thinking about that."

"Good," Alison said, relieved.

"See, they haven't thought of the part in a new way. But I'm sure that they would be open to a new interpretation. Especially if it was really great."

"I see what you mean, but maybe I should talk to them first. Before I start doing something they don't like."

"I think that would be a mistake."

"How can you say that?"

Jamie leaned forward. "See, as an actress, you've got to have a vision of the part."

"A vision?"

"I'll bet you don't even think of yourself as an actress."

"No, I don't really."

"You're just someone reading lines."

Alison nodded. It was amazing how well Jamie seemed to understand her.

"If you keep doing that, you're never going to be an actress. You have to know your character inside out. One way you can do that is to find out who she is, and say the lines the way she would. The way *she* would, not the way Kate wrote them, or Mr. Stephens wants you to say them."

Alison felt excited by what Jamie was saying, but scared, too. Jamie was right. All the great actresses understood how to mold a part, go beyond the lines that were written on a page. Alison knew she was too inexperienced to do the sort of thing that Jamie was talking about, but it certainly would be great to try. With Jamie's help, she could begin to do that. She'd feel like a real actress then.

Jamie gave Alison a long look. "I think we should run the lines again, only this time, I'll read Jane. You can get an idea of how I'd do the part if it was mine."

The girls spent the next hour doing just that. First Jamie read the part through, then it was Alison's turn. As she read, Alison saw places where she could bring her own ideas to the script. By the time they decided to take a break, she was flying high.

"I see exactly what you mean, Jamie. This feels like a whole new Jane," Alison said enthusiastically.

Jamie leaned back in her chair. *Mission accomplished,* she thought. Alison was going to walk into the studio with her "vision," a new, more intense Jane. It actually *was* a more interesting character the way Alison now played it, but it didn't fit into the story the same way. Her character, Wendy, was supposed to be the fiery one. Jamie was sure that Mr. Greenspan had picked Alison to play Jane because she looked as sweet as Jane in the script. He would hate it that Alison had taken it upon herself to change the part. And Rob Stephens, he'd go wild. Like Donna Wheeler had said, Rob was the kind of director who liked to keep a firm hand on his actors. He wouldn't appreciate Alison running off on her own like this.

The way Jamie saw it, they would probably fire Alison for not playing the role the way she was told to, especially if she started spouting off about making the role her own. That would be best. Alison gone, nice and neat.

Even if Mr. Greenspan and the others gave Alison another chance after they told her they hated the way she was playing Jane, Alison might be so confused and upset, she wouldn't be able to handle it. Then she'd probably leave on her own.

Jamie looked around the patio once more. Well, it wasn't like she was sending Alison back to such a horrible existence. As a matter of fact, if she had a choice, she'd let Alison stay on *Sticks and Stones,* and she'd become the Blakes' adopted daughter. Closing her eyes, Jamie began to plan once more. Now that Alison would be off the show, maybe she could persuade Mr. Greenspan and the others to replace Jane with another brother. Then Jamie would be the only girl on the show. That would be great.

"What are you smiling about?" Alison asked.

Jamie's eyes flew open. "What?"

"You were just lying there with a big smile on your face."

"Was I? I guess I was just feeling good. We did a lot today, and this pool is beautiful."

Alison got up and stretched. "Do you mind if I go for a swim? I was really tense while we were going over the script."

"Not at all. I'll just lie here," Jamie said, closing her eyes once more. She heard Alison dive into the pool, and was just drifting off toward sleep when she heard a voice say her name.

"Oh, hi, Steve," she said holding up her hand to block the glare of the sun. "And Brad. Were you two guys expected?"

Brad sat down on the lounge Alison had vacated. "We're always expected."

"Well, that must be nice for you," Jamie replied tartly. She didn't want him to think that she was some pushover like Alison. Still, she had to admit that he was incredibly cute. Today he was wearing a tight, sleeveless T-shirt and wild print surfer shorts. His hair was spiked, giving him a whole new look.

"I thought you and Alison were supposed to be working," Brad continued. "Some work."

"We've worked. Now we're taking a break."

"So it's okay if we stick around?" Steve said politely.

"Yeah, I think we're done for a while."

Alison popped out of the pool. "Hey, how did you know we'd be done by now?"

Brad shrugged. "I'm a master of timing."

As Alison toweled off, she wondered if Brad was here to see her or Jamie. He hadn't been around much at all since her party, though he had finally called and asked her to the prom. When she spoke to him last night and told him about her half day off and Jamie's plan to visit, he hadn't seemed especially interested, but now here he was. The way he and Jamie were looking at each other made Alison shiver slightly, though she tried to tell herself she just had a chill from the cool water.

"So how's the wonderful world of television?" Steve asked.

"Great," Alison replied. "Now that Jamie's been helping me with my part." She shot a smile in Jamie's direction.

"The pro's been giving you some pointers?" Brad said.

"I wouldn't say that," Jamie countered. "Alison's been doing a lot of work on her own."

"Really." Brad's tone was doubtful.

Alison wasn't sure that she liked Brad's attitude. Sure, she needed some help, but she wished Brad, of all people, had more confidence in her.

"You're sure you're not going to have to work on the day of the prom?" Brad asked.

"We tape on Friday nights. The prom's Saturday. I should be fine." Alison turned to Steve. "Have you asked anyone yet?"

Steve shook his head. "I guess there's not much point in asking Dana."

"I don't think so," Alison said softly. There was no reason to give Steve any encouragement. Besides, Dana would kill her if she did.

"What prom are you talking about?" Jamie inquired.

"Our junior prom," Steve said promptly. "It's coming up in couple of weeks."

"Oh," was Jamie's only comment. She had never been to a prom, or even a school dance for that matter. It was clear that Alison and her friends were much more into the high school scene than she'd ever been. Jamie had gone to class and then gone to work, never paying much attention to what extracurricular activities were going on in school.

One reason she stayed so aloof was embarrassment. She didn't want to get too close to anyone at school who might realize she used to be on television. Jamie assumed that her classmates would only feel sorry for the former Mimi, who was now treading the halls of an inner-city high school, just like they were. She didn't want anyone to know how poor she was, either.

Another reason Jamie was so out of the high school

scene was simply a matter of time. She needed to work as much as possible. She had obtained her work permit a year ago and had been piling up as many hours at the grocery store as she could. When she wasn't working, she was babysitting Elsie so that Mrs. O'Leary could take an extra shift at the restaurant. That didn't leave much time for dances or cheerleading tryouts.

Jamie looked at her watch. She had promised to be home early to babysit Elsie today, as a matter of fact. As usual, there was the sticky problem of getting home. Her mother had dropped her off earlier, but she was going to have to take a bus home. "I hate to break this up," Jamie said, "but I've got to get home."

"I'll drive you," Steve said. "Where do you live?"

Jamie hesitated. No one really knew where she lived, and she didn't want them to. It would be great to have a ride home, but it wasn't worth the risk of Steve being totally grossed out by her address.

"Don't you have to take Brad?" Jamie stalled.

"Oh, I can come by for him later." He turned to Brad. "You're going to want to spend some time with Alison anyway, aren't you?"

Brad shrugged. "I guess."

"Okay. I'll run you home, Jamie, and then I'll come back for Brad. How does that sound?"

Sounds like I'm trapped, Jamie said to herself, but out loud she said, "Give me a minute to change."

Grabbing her T-shirt and towel, Jamie headed into the house, trying to figure out what to do. She decided to have Steve drop her off on Melrose. Then, as she had on the day she'd gone shopping, she could just take the bus home.

As she got into Steve's terrific red sports car after she had said her good-byes to Alison and Brad, Jamie told Steve where she wanted to go.

He gunned the motor and pulled out of the driveway. "Do you live around there?" he asked conversationally.

"Sort of," she replied vaguely.

"I can wait if you want to do some shopping," Steve said politely. "I've got plenty of time."

Even though he was making this harder for her, Jamie appreciated the offer. "That's all right. I don't want to feel like I'm keeping you waiting."

"Hey, I'm waiting all the time."

"For what?" Jamie asked.

Steve shrugged. "For my life to begin."

"Oh, come on, Steve, it can't be that bad. Not with a car like this," she added jokingly.

"Even the car can't seem to get me a date with Dana."

"Well, what's so great about her?"

"You've met her."

"Yeah, I have. She's an okay girl, but there's plenty of other cool girls around."

"Right. And I bet none of them want to go out with me either."

Jamie shook her head. "Boy. You've got a bad case of the inferiors."

"There's something about me that turns girls off."

"Maybe it's the way you feel sorry for yourself." Jamie hadn't meant to be so blunt, and a quick glance in Steve's direction told her he was taking her remark badly.

"Thanks," he muttered. "I knew my looks weren't so hot, but I didn't think my personality stunk too."

"That's not what I said, Steve."

"Close enough."

Jamie wasn't a redhead for nothing. She could feel herself getting angry. What was it with these rich kids anyway? Didn't they realize how lucky they were? Steve had the coolest car in the world, he was obviously bright, and even cute in a different sort of way. Moreover, he was nice, not a quality a lot of sixteen-year-old boys possessed, at least in her experience. But here he was crying and moaning because he couldn't get a date with a twit like Dana.

"Steve, snap out of it!" she finally said.

"Huh?"

"You're not exactly hamburger meat, but the way you complain about yourself, people are going to think you are. Girl people," Jamie emphasized. "Maybe if you had a better self-image, Dana would be after *you.*"

Steve glanced at her hopefully. "You mean I should act as if she would be lucky to get me."

"Exactly."

Turning his attention back to the road, Steve was quiet for a minute. Then he said, "But that won't work. I mean, there would have to be some reason why my image would improve."

"What about this hot new car?"

"Hasn't snowed her yet."

"Well," Jamie improvised, "find some other girl to take to the dance. Someone she'll get jealous of. It's the oldest trick in the book."

Steve hit the brakes at a red light. "Great idea!"

"Hey, it was a good thing I was wearing my seat belt, I almost . . ."

"Will you go with me?"

"What!"

"You'd make any girl jealous."

What had she gotten into now? She didn't want Steve to drop her off at home, she certainly didn't want him to pick her up there for a date. "Uh . . ."

"Look," Steve said reasonably. "You don't have to tell me right now. Why don't you think about it?"

Jamie really didn't have a good answer to that.

Steve pulled over to the curb. "You wanted to get off at this corner?"

"Yeah, this will be great. I'll let you know about the prom, okay?"

Steve smiled at her. "I'll wait."

Jamie got out of the car and walked into one of the stores on Melrose. When she was sure Steve was gone, she went outside and waited at the bus stop. If this show seemed like a hit at all, Jamie promised herself, she was going to move as soon as possible. It might be fun to go to the prom with Steve, if only he could pick her up someplace halfway decent.

Jamie got off the bus a few blocks from her apartment. She was already late. Her mother had a dental appointment, and Jamie hoped that she wasn't going to be late. Hurrying, she climbed the stairs and turned her key in the lock. As she opened the door, her eyes widened in shock.

Her voice shaking, she asked, "What are you doing here?"

Chapter 10

Mr. O'Leary lifted Elsie from his lap. "Go play in the bedroom, honey. I want to talk to your sister."

Elsie looked from her father to Jamie. "What's wrong?"

Jamie came over and gave her a quick hug. "Nothing. I just haven't seen Dad in a while."

Elsie, looking worried, picked up her doll and took it into the bedroom.

"Where's Mom?" Jamie asked testily.

"She went to the dentist."

"How long have you been here?" she demanded.

"All afternoon. What are you so upset about, Jamie?"

Jamie stared at her father. He had certainly made himself at home. His suit jacket was flung across the back of the couch, and his tie was loosened. She was surprised to see how much older he looked since his last visit. Her father's thinning hair was now more gray

than blond, and the lines that used to crease his fore-
head when he smiled or frowned now seemed to be
there permanently.

"Why are you looking at me like that?" Mr.
O'Leary asked uncomfortably.

Jamie straightened up and ignored his question. "I
asked you when I came in what you're doing here."

"I told you on the phone I was coming."

"Where are you staying?"

"I don't know yet. I thought maybe . . ."

"Not here."

"Don't you think that's up to your mother to decide?"

"Not really. I live here, too. I help pay the rent," she
said pointedly.

"Jamie, I don't know why you're so angry all the
time. Maybe I haven't been the best father—"

"You got that right," Jamie said bitterly.

"But I want you to give me another chance."

Jamie turned away and began straightening the
room.

"Your sister doesn't have any trouble with me being
back."

"My sister is four."

"Well, your mom doesn't seem to, either."

Jamie just shook her head. Her father was right. It
was pretty clear that her mother still cared. If this was
love, Jamie didn't think she wanted any part of it.

"I think things can work out better this time,
Jamie."

"Why? Because I'm working again?"

"That's part of it," Mr. O'Leary admitted. "I'm sure I can help you."

"I have an agent now, Meg Wildman. I don't need you to manage my career anymore."

"Then I'll find something else to do. But at least we can all be together."

Jamie sat on the chair across from him. "I don't want us to be together. Not if together includes you."

She could tell how much she hurt him. The look on his face was the same one people got when they were punched in the stomach. A tiny thread of dismay pulled through her, but Jamie ignored it. He felt terrible? Well, tough. How many nights had she gone to sleep feeling alone and abandoned? The least she could do was show him how that felt.

In her heart though, Jamie knew that she couldn't fight him and her mother. If Mrs. O'Leary wanted him back, back he would probably come. That didn't mean she had to like it, though. And that didn't mean her father had to be a permanent fixture in her life. Jamie was about to get Alison Blake removed from *Sticks and Stones.* Maybe she could make her father disappear, too.

Alison looked around the set of the Stickleys' kitchen. It was so weird to see a television stage set in real life. She could look over at the monitor, just a few feet away, and the room looked like an ordinary kitchen. But as soon as Alison turned away, she saw that the supposedly wooden table was made out of some kind of cheap plyboard, and the kitchen cabinets had no backs. A fine layer of sawdust from the recent assembly lay over the counters, but you couldn't see that on the small screen either.

Donna Wheeler came up to her and followed Alison's gaze. "Amazing, isn't it?" she said. "I worked on a soap opera once where I played a debutante who lived in a mansion. The velvet on the chairs was cracked, and there was dust everywhere, but on TV, the interior decoration looked like a million bucks."

"It's all illusion," Alison said.

Donna shrugged. "You've had a week to learn that."

Alison felt like a silly kid. Of course, she knew it was all make-believe. Or did she? Alison had to admit she was so into her part that perhaps she really did expect the Stickleys to have a real kitchen.

"Are you excited about our first dress rehearsal?"

"I wouldn't exactly say excited is the right word," Alison said glumly.

Donna laughed. "Don't worry, we all feel the same way. But you've been doing fine. You shouldn't have any problems."

Alison murmured her thanks. What Donna didn't know was that she and Jamie had chosen this first dress rehearsal to unveil the new, improved Jane. It had been difficult working on her new interpretation at night, while still doing the old one during the day. Jamie thought that the feistier Jane would make more of an impression when she was in costume, and Alison had to agree.

Telling Donna she wanted to get some hot tea for her throat, Alison left the set and walked to the commissary. She was having second and third thoughts about what she was about to do. Everyone said she was doing a good job. Donna had just told her she was fine. Why change things now?

Still, she had to admit that her new spin on the role was exciting. She wanted to try it out, if she could just dig up the nerve. As she got her tea, Alison thought about how encouraging Jamie had been, always there with a helpful word or a good suggestion. If Alison didn't put their changes into effect, Jamie would be terribly disappointed in her.

Spotting Mike sitting at one of the tables, Alison took her tea and went to sit down beside him. "Set for the dress rehearsal?"

"Ready as I'll ever be," he said with a slight smile. "Dan seems happy, don't you think?"

Alison nodded. "Everyone is excited."

"I don't know what it will be like to tape in front of an audience tomorrow. I've never done anything like that before."

Mike looked scared. It seemed odd for her to reassure him, but Alison smiled at him, and said, "Hey, they don't give the death sentence for bad performances."

"Just the pink slip."

She hadn't spent much time talking to Mike.

Whenever they had a few moments on a break or at lunch, Jamie always seemed to be around. It would be interesting to get to know him better. Mike was such a great-looking guy, and a good actor, too. Yet, he never seemed very happy. Alison wondered why.

Should she mention she was going to be changing the way she was going to do her part? Alison was about to tell Mike, so she wouldn't throw his timing off, when he said, "Did you know we have a new director?"

"What!"

"Rob Stephens is gone."

"He got fired?"

"No. He got tapped to direct a movie."

"Then who's going to direct us?" Alison asked, in something of a panic.

"Hey, hey." Mike patted her hand. "No big deal. A guy named Kevin Voight is going to do it. He's a pro, so there's no problem."

"Maybe he won't mind if I change the way I'm playing my part."

"What?" Mike looked at her in amazement.

"I just came up with a new concept for the role," Alison said vaguely.

Before Mike could respond, Jamie came up to them.

"What's all this about? Something wrong?" There was a frown on her face as she noticed Mike's hand on Alison's.

"Did you hear we have a new director?" Alison asked.

"You're kidding." Jamie shook her head as Mike repeated his news. Then Mike said, "And it appears that Alison has decided to change the way she's going to interpret her role."

Jamie didn't want Mike to know that she was responsible. "So?" she said neutrally.

Mike continued, "I think we should try and talk her out of it, Jamie. She could blow everything."

Darn you, Mike, Jamie thought to herself. But all she said was, "It might be a good idea."

"It might be a disaster." Mike stared at Jamie for a long, hard minute. "For Alison and anyone else involved."

Jamie was let off the hook by one of the script girls, who came up to them and said, "They're calling the rehearsal a few minutes early. Dan wants you back on the set."

Alison and Jamie walked back to the set silently, each lost in her own thoughts.

Maybe Mike's right, Alison thought worriedly. *I am going out on a big limb here.*

Maybe Mike's right. Jamie bit her lip. *He's already figured out I had something to do with this. Who cares if Alison gets kicked off the show if I'm gone, too?*

By the time they arrived on the set, most of the cast and crew had gathered around Dan.

"As some of you may have heard," Dan began, "Rob Stephens had an excellent opportunity to direct a movie, and he took it. But not to worry, our new director, Kevin Voight, has years of experience working on sitcoms, and since Rob told me earlier this might be happening, we invited Kevin on the set to watch us reading our lines. Now, of course, he'll be taking over, and I want you to know I have complete confidence in him." Mr. Greenspan turned to Kevin. "Want to say a few words?"

"Well, troops," Kevin said, running a hand through his short, curly hair, "I hope you don't mind the change in personnel. You haven't had too long to get used to Rob, so that's good." He laughed. "I think the first thing we should do is have our dress rehearsal. Then, I'll be better prepared to talk to you individually and as a group about where the show is at. We are scheduled to tape tomorrow, first another dress rehearsal before an audience, and then the actual show in front of a different group. If I see anything radically wrong with today's dress, we can postpone the taping . . ." he turned to Dan Greenspan, who nodded, "but from what I've seen so far, we shouldn't have any problems."

Other than me, Alison said silently. She turned to Jamie, who wasn't moving, even though the rest of the group was hurrying off to change into their costumes. "What's wrong?" she asked.

"Nothing," Jamie snapped.

"Well, excuse me."

"Sorry. I just don't like surprises. A new director is definitely a surprise."

"It shouldn't make that much difference, should it?"

"I don't know."

The girls started walking toward the dressing room. "You know, maybe this is a sign I shouldn't fiddle with my part," Alison began.

Jamie hesitated. "You could be right."

"Do you think so? You were so sure."

"We could both be in a lot of trouble," Jamie muttered.

There was a long silence as the girls walked into their dressing room and began changing into their costumes. "Jamie, I'm going to play it the way you and I practiced," Alison finally said.

Now it was Jamie's turn to be worried. "Are you sure?"

"I know it's better this way, and you must think so. You've told me so over and over."

"Yes, but . . ."

"I'll just try it. If Kevin hates it, I can change back."

"Why take the chance?"

Alison thought about it. "I've never taken many chances. Now that I've started, I have to admit, it feels pretty good."

Jamie shrugged. "All right, if you think that's what you want to do." Maybe this would go according to plan after all. Jamie could only hope.

Alison finished buttoning her blouse. "I guess we better get out there."

Even though there were empty chairs instead of an audience, an air of expectation had settled over everyone involved in *Sticks and Stones*. Just being in costume and makeup made everything seem different.

When she got out on the stage, Alison glanced around at the people she had been working with all week. Now, they really were the Stickleys and Stones. Only Rodney, who wasn't that far removed from his character, seemed familiar.

"Places everyone," the assistant director called.

That meant her and Mike in the kitchen. "Break a leg," Mike whispered as they moved on stage.

She looked at him, startled.

"It's a show business expression for good luck."

"Oh. Thanks. Break a leg, yourself."

There was so much to remember, where to move, what to say, and of course, how to say it, Alison wasn't sure she could do any of it. But before she realized it, every scene was completed, and the dress rehearsal ended. Well, she had done it her way. Nervously, she looked at Jamie. They hadn't had any scenes together, and Alison wanted to know what Jamie had thought of her performance. Jamie gave her a big okay sign.

Alison sighed with relief.

Jamie had to admit that Alison had done a good job, and that knowledge evoked a lot of mixed feelings in her. But how would the powers that be feel about it?

The group of actors and actresses stood huddled together, no one saying a word, though Alison noticed Donna and Ben were giving her odd glances. Kevin and Dan hurried down from the control room.

"Well," said Kevin. "I think we all got through that in one piece." He looked around at the crew. "Thanks, guys and gals. I'll talk to you later. Right now, I'm going to have one-on-one conferences with the cast." He turned his attention to Alison. "Starting with you."

Jamie watched nervously as Alison was marched off between Kevin and Mr. Greenspan. Well, it was all going to hit the fan now.

As soon as Alison was out of earshot, the rest of the cast started discussing her.

"She changed everything," Ben said, perplexed.

"But it was very interesting," Donna replied.

Rodney shook his head. "I didn't know we were allowed to do that."

Jamie looked at Mike. "What did you think?"

"I've been thinking about this. Personally, I don't think Alison Blake is brave enough to reinvent her part all on her own." He cast a hard stare in Jamie's direction. "But I do think the new interpretation is an improvement. It would have helped, though, if we all had more time to get used to it, with it so close to taping and all."

Jamie didn't respond to that. She was too busy worrying about what was going on in Mr. Greenspan's office.

Dan Greenspan, his hands folded on his desk, was looking at Alison, perplexed. "Alison, what was going on out there? You haven't read like that all week."

"Well, Mr. Greenspan, I've been working on this new interpretation." Now, with Dan, Kevin, and Kate Morton staring at her, that explanation sounded incredibly weak, even to her own ears.

"Why didn't you come to one of us and tell us that's what you had in mind?" Kate asked.

All the reasons for secrecy that had seemed so good and logical seemed to have flown out of her head. "I don't know," she replied helplessly.

"You don't know?" Kate repeated.

Alison tried to muster what was left of her confidence. "I just thought I could make the part my own. I thought I could bring something new to Jane."

"It was new all right," Mr. Greenspan said.

Alison clenched her hands together. "Look, I'm terribly sorry. I'll do it the old way."

"You do remember the old way?" Mr. Greenspan asked dryly.

"Of course. And I'll never do anything like this again. Really." She was going to be fired, she just knew it.

Kevin held up his hand. "Wait a minute. I think Alison is onto something."

"You do?" Kate asked.

Dan looked surprised as well.

"Sure. Let's think about this for a minute. We still want to keep the character of Jane likable and innocent, but she doesn't have to be a total goody-goody. That would be boring. I think what Alison did added some spice."

Mr. Greenspan looked at Kate, who shrugged. "I can see his point," she said. "We don't want the girls too much alike, but perhaps Jane was coming across a little bland. We were so taken aback by the change, maybe we haven't seen how it can work."

"We still keep Jane as the nicer one," Kevin said, "but we give her dimension. I think that's all Alison was trying to do."

Sitting back in his leather chair, Mr. Greenspan nodded. "Very clever, actually. Alison's shaped this role, punched it up, and all on her own, too." He flopped forward looking Alison right in the eye. "Of course, next time, we might like just a hint of what you're up to."

"Oh yes, yes," Alison stuttered. Then she asked, "You mean you like it?"

The adults laughed. "I guess we do," Kate said, "although that's not what was in my mind as I was watching your performance."

"Good," Alison said with relief. "Jamie will be so glad."

"Jamie?" Kevin asked.

"She helped me every step of the way."

Mr. Greenspan smiled at her benignly. "Isn't that terrific? So often there is rivalry between two actresses on a television show. I think it's wonderful that you two are so close, so *there* for each other." He turned to Kate. "And their relationship will make for great publicity, too," he added with a wink.

Whew. Alison could hardly believe it. They had actually liked what she'd done. She felt elated, excited, and exhausted all at the same time. Wait 'til she told Jamie.

———

As she got ready for bed that night, Jamie tried to recall if she had ever had a day with more ups and downs in her life. Daddy dearest was staying at a nearby motel for the moment, but it was clear he was sticking around. Then, Alison turned out to be the creative genius of *Sticks and Stones*.

Spitting her toothpaste into the sink, she thought for the millionth time what a bad break it was that Rob Stephens had left the show. He would have hated the new Jane, Jamie was sure of that. Why, Alison had even told her it was Kevin who convinced Dan and Kate that this whole new Jane was a good idea.

Jamie sighed. Well, at least she had gotten brownie points for helping Alison with her role. Dan, Kate, and Kevin had all told her what a great job she'd done and how pleased they were she was coaching her less-experienced co-star. She guessed she had to thank Alison for singing her praises. Jamie turned off the bathroom light. *Alison,* she thought. Well, it was clear Alison was going to be around for a while. Jamie supposed she'd just have to make the best of it. Jamie shivered a little as she pulled the covers up over her. What if things had gone differently? She and Alison could *both* have been out.

Stop thinking, Jamie told herself. *You've got to get your beauty sleep. Tomorrow's the big day, shooting in front of a live audience.*

As she drifted off, Jamie thought about Alison in her big house and gorgeous bedroom. Was she getting any sleep?

Alison stood at her window, brushing her hair. No matter how exciting tomorrow was, and it was sure to be incredible, she had a feeling she would always remember this day more. It had taken a lot of courage to shake up her role. Of course, she never would have, could have, done it without Jamie.

Jamie. She had wanted to help her, hadn't she? Alison tried to block out the niggling doubts that kept floating around her head. Jamie had looked almost disappointed when Alison came out of her meeting with Dan and the others, flying high. *No,* she told herself firmly. Jamie might have a chip on her shoulder as big as a boulder, but Alison was sure she had the good of the show at heart.

She put her brush down on the dresser. Everyone was coming to the taping tomorrow. Her parents, Dana, Steve, and of course Brad. Probably each one of them at one time or another had doubted she could actually do this. Alison smiled as she turned toward her bed. She was doing it just fine.

Official Rules:

1. Mail your entry to "Hollywood Wars Sweepstakes," Puffin Books Marketing Dept., Penguin USA, 375 Hudson St., New York, NY 10014. One entry per person.

2. Entries must be received by Nov. 30, 1993. Puffin Books is not responsible for lost or misdirected mail.

3. Winner will be chosen in a random drawing. Winner will be notified by mail.

4. This contest is open to all US and Canadian residents between the ages of 8 and 18 as of January 1, 1993. Void where prohibited. Employees of Penguin USA (and their families), their respective affiliates, retailers, distributors, and advertising, promotion and production agencies are not eligible.

5. Taxes, if any, are the responsibility of the prize winner. Winner's parents/guardians will be required to sign and return a statement of eiligibility. Names and addresses of the winner and companions may be used for promotional purposes.

6. If another minor is to accompany the winner, the parents/guardians of that minor will be required to sign and return the same forms. Winner and any companion who may be a minor must be accompanied by a legal guardian.

7. Travel and accommodations (based on triple occupancy) are subject to space and departure availability. Reservations, once made, are final and cannot be rescheduled. Certain travel restrictions may apply, including specific blackout dates during peak travel periods. No substitution or transfer of prize is permitted. Winner and companions are responsible for providing their own transportation to and from the airport.

8. For the name of the prize-winner, send a self-addressed, stamped envelope to: "Hollywood Wars Sweepstakes," Puffin Marketing Dept., Penguin USA, 375 Hudson St., New York, NY 10014.

● ● ● ● ● ● ● ● ● ● ● ● ● ● ● ● ● ● ●

Win a trip for three to Hollywood, California or New York City!

Puffin is pleased to announce the Hollywood Wars Sweepstakes.

Just fill out this entry blank, and send it in before November 30, 1993. You must be between the ages of 8 and 18 to enter.

Mail this form to:
Hollywood Wars Sweepstakes
Puffin Books Marketing Dept.
Penguin USA
375 Hudson Street
New York, NY 10014

NAME_____ AGE_____

ADDRESS_____

CITY/STATE/ZIP_____

PHONE_____

● ● ● ● ● ● ● ● ● ● ● ● ● ● ● ● ● ● ●